Penguin Books
Maigret Mystified

D1394198

Georges Simenon was born at Liège in
Belgium in 1903. At sixteen he began
work as a journalist on the *Gazette de
Liège*. He has published over 175 books,
many of them psychological novels, and
others in the Inspector Maigret series, and
his work has been admired by almost all
the leading French and English critics.
His books have been translated into more
than twenty-five languages and more than
forty of them have been filmed; his
psychological novels have had a great
influence on the French cinema. He has
travelled all over the world, and at one
time lived in a cutter making long
journeys of exploration round the coasts
of Northern Europe. He is married and
has four children. His recreations are
riding, fishing, and golf.

Georges Simenon

Maigret Mystified

Translated by Jean Stewart

Penguin Books

Penguin Books Ltd, Harmondsworth,
Middlesex, England
Penguin Books Inc., 7110 Ambassador Road,
Baltimore, Maryland 21207, U.S.A.
Penguin Books Australia Ltd,
Ringwood, Victoria, Australia

L'Ombre chinoise first published in 1932
First published in Great Britain,
under the title The Shadow in the Courtyard
in The Triumph of Inspector Maigret,
by Hurst & Blackett 1934
This translation first published in
Penguin Books 1964
Reprinted 1966, 1970, 1972

Copyright © A. Fayard et Cie, 1932
Translation copyright © Jean Stewart, 1964

Made and printed in Great Britain by
C. Nicholls & Company Ltd
Set in Monotype Garamond

Contents

Chapter 1

The Shadow Against the Window

It was ten o'clock at night. The iron gates of the garden were shut, the Place des Vosges deserted, with gleaming car tracks on the asphalt and the unbroken murmur of the fountains, the leafless trees and the monotonous outline of identical roofs silhouetted against the sky.

Under the arcades which form a tremendous girdle round the Square there were few lights. Only in three or four shops. Inspector Maigret saw a family eating in one of them, amidst a clutter of beaded funeral wreaths.

He tried to read the numbers over the doors, but he had scarcely got beyond the shop with the wreaths when a small female figure emerged from the darkness.

'Are you the person I spoke to on the telephone?'

She must have been keeping watch for a long time. In spite of the November chill, she was wearing no coat over her apron. Her nose was red and her eyes worried.

Less than a hundred yards away, at the corner of the rue de Béarn, a uniformed policeman was on duty.

'Didn't you tell him?' grumbled Maigret.

'No! because of Madame de Saint-Marc, who's having a baby.... Look, there's the doctor's car. They've had to send for him in a hurry....'

Three cars were parked beside the pavement, with their sidelights on and rear lamps glowing red. There was an uncertain pallor about the sky, where clouds drifted over a moon-drenched expanse; almost a hint of snow in the air.

The concierge turned in under the arched entrance to

the block of flats, which was lit by a dusty twenty-five-watt lamp.

'I'll explain.... Here's the courtyard.... You have to cross it to get into any part of the house, except the two shops.... This is my lodge on the left.... Don't take any notice ... I hadn't time to put the children to bed....'

There were two of them in the untidy kitchen, a boy and a girl. But the concierge did not go in there. She pointed out a long building at the far end of the spacious, well-proportioned courtyard.

'It's there.... Now you'll understand....'

Maigret looked with some curiosity at this odd little woman, whose fluttering hands betrayed her excitement.

'Somebody's asking to speak to an inspector on the phone', he had been told a short while ago at Police Headquarters.

He heard a muffled voice. He repeated three or four times:

'Speak up! ... I can't hear you! ...'

'I can't ... I'm speaking from the tobacconist's ... so ...'

And then a rambling message.

'Somebody must come along at once to 61 Place des Vosges.... Yes ... I think there's been a crime.... But don't let anybody know yet! ...'

And now the concierge was pointing to the tall windows on the first floor. Behind the curtains, shadows could be seen moving to and fro.

'That's where ...'

'The crime?'

'No! Madame de Saint-Marc having her baby.... Her first.... She's not very strong.... You understand? ...'

And the courtyard was even darker than the Place des Vosges. It was lit by a single lamp, fixed to the wall. There seemed to be a staircase behind a glazed door, and here and there lighted windows.

'But what about the crime?'

'Well! At six o'clock, the staff of Couchet's went home. . . .'

'One minute. What's Couchet's?'

'The building at the end. . . . A laboratory where they make serums. . . . You must have heard of them . . . Dr Rivière's Serums. . . .'

'That lighted window?'

'Wait a minute. . . . Today's the 30th. . . . So Monsieur Couchet was there. . . . He generally stays behind by himself when the office is closed . . . I saw him through the window, sitting in his armchair. . . . Look . . .'

A window with frosted panes. A strange shadow, like that of a man slumped forward on his desk.

'Is that him?'

'Yes. . . . About eight o'clock, when I went to empty my dustbin, I happened to glance up. . . . He was writing . . . you could see his hand holding a pen or a pencil. . . .'

'What time did the crime . . .'

'Just a moment! I went upstairs to get news of Madame de Saint-Marc. . . . I looked up again when I was coming downstairs. . . . He was just like he is now, and I even thought he must have fallen asleep –'

Maigret was beginning to grow impatient.

' – then a quarter of an hour later . . .'

'Yes, yes! He was still in the same place! Get to the point. . . .'

'That's all . . . I wanted to find out. . . . I knocked at the door of his office. . . . There was no answer so I went in. . . . He's dead. There's blood all over the place. . . .'

'Why didn't you inform the police station? It's close by, in the rue de Béarn. . . .'

'And they'd all have come along in uniform and

disturbed the whole house! I told you Madame de Saint-Marc ...'

Maigret had both hands in his pockets and his pipe between his teeth. He looked up at the first-floor windows and got the impression that the event was imminent, for the bustle was increasing. A door was heard opening, footsteps coming downstairs. A tall, broad silhouette appeared in the courtyard and the concierge, touching the Inspector's arm, murmured respectfully:

'That's Monsieur de Saint-Marc.... He's a former ambassador....'

The man, whose face could not be seen clearly, halted, took a few steps and then stopped again, keeping his eyes fixed on his own windows.

'They must have sent him outside.... As they did a little while back.... Come on ... Oh dear, there they go again with their gramophone, just above the Saint-Marcs! ...'

A smaller window on the second floor, less brightly lit. It was closed, and the music could be guessed at rather than heard.

The concierge, angular, nervous, red-eyed, her fingers fluttering, went to the far end of the courtyard and pointed to a small flight of steps and a half-open door.

'You'll see him, on your left.... I'd rather not go back there ...'

A very ordinary sort of office, with light-coloured furniture and plain wall-paper.

And a man of forty-five, sitting in an armchair, with his head lying on the papers strewn in front of him. He had been shot through the chest.

Maigret listened attentively: the concierge was still outside, waiting for him, and Monsieur de Saint-Marc was still walking up and down in the courtyard. From time to time a bus passed through the square and its clatter intensified the silence that followed.

The Inspector touched nothing. He merely made sure that the weapon had not been left in the office, stood looking about him for three or four minutes, puffing gently at his pipe, then went out, with a stubborn look on his face.

'Well?'

The concierge was still there. She spoke in a whisper.

'Nothing! He's dead.'

'They've just sent for Monsieur de Saint-Marc up there. . . .'

There was much coming and going in the apartment. Doors slammed. Somebody ran.

'She's so delicate!'

'Oh, sure!' grunted Maigret, scratching the back of his neck. 'Only we're not concerned with that. Have you any idea who could have gone into the office?'

'Me? How could I? . . .'

'Please! You must be able to see the tenants go past from your lodge.'

'I ought to be able to! If the landlord would give me a decent lodge, and wasn't so stingy about lighting. . . . I'm only just able to hear footsteps and make out shadows at night. . . . There are some footsteps I can recognize. . . .'

'And you've noticed nothing unusual since six o'clock?'

'Nothing! Almost all the tenants came down to empty their rubbish. . . . That's the place, to the left of my lodge – you see those three dustbins? . . . They aren't supposed to come before seven o'clock in the evening. . . .'

'And nobody came in through the entrance?'

'How d'you expect me to know? . . . You obviously don't know the building. There are twenty-eight tenants . . . not to speak of Couchet's, where they're coming and going the whole time. . . .'

There were steps in the entrance. A man wearing a bowler hat came into the courtyard, turned left and, going towards the dustbins, picked up an empty one. In spite of the darkness he must have caught sight of Maigret and the concierge, for he stood still a moment, and said at last:

'Nothing for me?'

'Nothing, Monsieur Martin....'

And Maigret inquired:

'Who's that?'

'An official in the Wills and Probate Office, Monsieur Martin, who lives on the second floor with his wife.'

'How does his dustbin happen to be ...'

'They nearly all do that when they have to go out. They bring them down when they leave and collect them when they come in again.... Did you hear that?'

'What?'

'I thought ... it sounded like a baby's cry.... If only those two up there would stop their wretched gramophone!... Of course they're perfectly well aware that Madame de Saint-Marc's having a baby....'

She rushed towards the staircase as somebody came down.

'Well, doctor?... Is it a boy?...'

'A girl.'

And the doctor went out. His car was heard starting up and driving away.

The house went on living its ordinary life. The dark courtyard. The entrance with its feeble lamp. The lighted windows and the dimly heard music of a gramophone.

The dead man was still in his office, all alone, with his head among the scattered letters.

Suddenly a cry rang out from the second floor. A piercing cry, like a desperate call for help. But the concierge did not even give a start, merely sighing as she pushed open the door of her lodge:

'Oh dear, that madwoman again. . . .'

Then she uttered a cry herself, because one of her children had broken a plate. In the light, Maigret saw a thin, tired face, a body of indeterminate age.

'When are all the formalities going to start?' she asked.

The *tabac* opposite was still open, and a few minutes later Maigret had shut himself up in the telephone booth. He too lowered his voice as he gave his instructions.

'Yes. . . . Get the Parquet. . . . 61. . . . It's almost at the corner of the rue de Turenne. . . . And let them know at the Technical Branch. . . . Hello? . . . Yes, I'll stay on the spot. . . .'

He took a few steps along the pavement, made his way mechanically through the entrance, and finally took up his post in the middle of the courtyard, sullenly hunching his shoulders because of the cold.

The lights in the windows began to go out. The dead man's shadow could still be seen silhouetted against the frosted glass.

A taxi stopped. Not the Parquet yet. A young woman hurried across the courtyard, leaving a trail of scent behind her, and pushed open the door of the office.

Chapter 2

A Real Good Sort

There followed a series of misunderstandings which led to an absurd situation. The young woman, on discovering the corpse, swung round. She caught sight of Maigret's tall figure framed in the doorway. The association of ideas was automatic: here was a dead man, there stood the murderer.

And with staring eyes and shrinking limbs, she opened her mouth wide to call for help, letting go of her handbag.

Maigret had no time to argue. He seized her by the arm and put his hand over her mouth.

'Hush! ... You're making a mistake! ... Police! ...'

Failing at first to grasp the meaning of the words, she went on struggling like the highly-strung creature that she was, tried to bite, kicked out backwards.

There was a sound of tearing silk: the shoulder-strap of her dress.

And at last things calmed down. Maigret repeated:

'No noise. ... I'm a policeman. ... There's no need to wake up the house. ...'

The salient feature of this crime was the unusual silence and calm that prevailed, as the twenty-eight tenants of the house went on living their normal lives with a corpse in their midst.

The young woman was trying to fix her dress.

'Were you his mistress?'

A sullen glare at Maigret, while she hunted for a pin to fasten her strap.

'Had you a date with him tonight?'

'Eight o'clock at the Select. . . . We were to dine together and go on to the theatre. . . .'

'When he failed to turn up at eight o'clock, didn't you telephone?'

'Yes! I was told the receiver had been left off the hook.'

They both caught sight of it simultaneously, on the desk. The man must have knocked it over as he fell forward.

Footsteps in the courtyard, where the slightest sounds were amplified that night as though under a sounding-board. The concierge called out from the threshold, so as not to see the corpse:

'Inspector, it's the district police. . . .'

She had no fondness for them. They came along, four or five of them, making no effort to conceal their presence. One of them was finishing a funny story. Another inquired, as he reached the office:

'Where's the corpse?'

As the District Inspector was away, his clerk had replaced him, and Maigret was the more readily able to keep control of operations.

'Leave your men outside. I'm waiting for the Parquet. It's better that the tenants should suspect nothing. . . .'

And while the clerk was looking round the office, he turned to the young woman once more.

'What's your name?'

'Nine . . . Nine Moinard, but I'm always called Nine. . . .'

'Have you known Couchet a long time?'

'About six months. . . .'

There was no need to ask her many questions. To watch her was enough. A pretty girl, still fairly inexperienced. She was obviously dressed by a good couturier. But her style of make-up, the way she held her bag and gloves and looked aggressively at people, betrayed the music-hall artist.

'A dancer?'

'I was at the Moulin Bleu. . . .'

'And now?'

'I'm with him. . . .'

She had not had time to weep. It had all happened too quickly and as yet she had not a very clear grasp of the true situation.

'Did he live with you?'

'Not really, as he's married. . . . But still. . . .'

'Your address?'

'Hôtel Pigalle. . . . Rue Pigalle. . . .'

The clerk observed:

'They can't talk of burglary, in any case!'

'Why?'

'Look! The safe's behind him! It's not locked, but the dead man's back would stop anyone from opening the door.'

Nine, who had pulled a tiny handkerchief from her bag, was sniffling and dabbing her nostrils.

A minute later the atmosphere had changed. Cars braked outside, footsteps and voices rang out in the courtyard Then there were handshakes, questions, noisy conversations. The Parquet people had come. The police doctor was examining the body and the photographers were setting up their cameras.

For Maigret this was a trying moment to be endured. He said the few things that had to be said, and then went down into the courtyard with his hands in his pockets, lit his pipe, and ran into somebody in the darkness. It was the concierge, who could not resign herself to letting strangers wander about in her house without finding out what they were up to.

'What's your name?' Maigret asked her in a friendly tone.

'Madame Bourcier. . . . Are those gentlemen going to

stay much longer?... Look, the light's gone out in Madame de Saint-Marc's room.... She must have fallen asleep, poor thing....'

As he examined the house, the Inspector noticed another light, a cream-coloured curtain and behind it a woman's silhouette. She was small and thin, like the concierge. Her voice could not be heard, but it was obvious that she was in a temper. Sometimes she stood stock still, staring at somebody who could not be seen. Then suddenly she would start talking and gesticulating, and would take a few steps forward.

'Who's that?'

'Madame Martin.... You saw her husband coming home just now.... You know, the one who took up his dustbin.... The official from Wills and Probate....'

'Do they often quarrel?'

'They don't quarrel.... She's the one who does all the shouting.... He daren't even open his mouth....'

From time to time Maigret cast a glance into the office, where some ten men were bustling about. From the doorway, the examining magistrate called out to the concierge.

'Who's in charge of the firm, after Monsieur Couchet?'

'The managing director, Monsieur Philippe. He lives not far away, in the Île Saint-Louis....'

'Is he on the telephone?'

'Surely....'

A man's voice was heard telephoning. Upstairs, Madame Martin's silhouette was no longer visible against the curtain. On the other hand, an odd-looking figure came down the stairs, crossed the courtyard stealthily, and made off down the street. Maigret recognized the bowler hat and buff overcoat of Monsieur Martin.

It was midnight. The gramophone-playing girls put out their light. Apart from the offices, the only room still lighted was the Saint-Marcs' drawing-room on the first floor, where the former ambassador and the midwife were talking in low tones, amid a sickly hospital smell.

In spite of the lateness of the hour, Monsieur Philippe, when he appeared, was spick and span, his dark beard neat and trim, and grey suede gloves on his hands. He was a man of about forty, a typical serious, well-bred intellectual.

True, he was astonished and even shocked by the news. But there seemed a sort of reservation in his emotion.

'Considering the life he led . . .' he sighed.

'What sort of life?'

'I'm never going to say anything against Monsieur Couchet. In any case, there's nothing to be said against him. He was free to do what he liked with his time.'

'One moment! Did Monsieur Couchet run the business himself?'

'Not even indirectly. He started it off, but once it had got going he left me entire responsibility. So much so that I sometimes didn't see him for a fortnight. Only today, for instance, I waited for him till five o'clock. Tomorrow is pay-day. Monsieur Couchet was to bring me the necessary funds for the staff's wages. About three hundred thousand francs. At five o'clock I had to go and I left him a report on his desk.'

It was found there, a typewritten sheet lying under the dead man's hand. A routine report: proposals for increasing one clerk's salary and dismissing one of the delivery-men, publicity plans for Latin-American countries. . . .

'So that the three hundred thousand francs should be here?' asked Maigret.

'In the safe. The proof of that is that Monsieur Couchet had opened it. He and I were the only two who had the key and the combination. . . .'

But in order to open the safe the body would have to be moved, and so they waited for the photographers to have completed their job. The police doctor made his statement. Couchet had been shot through the chest and, the aorta having been pierced, death had been instantaneous. The shot had probably been fired from about three yards. The bullet was of the commonest calibre: 6-mm. ·35.

Monsieur Philippe was explaining things to the examining magistrate.

'We only had our labs here in the Place des Vosges, they are behind this office.'

He opened a door, and disclosed a large room with a glazed roof where thousands of test-tubes stood in rows. Behind another door Maigret thought he heard a noise.

'What's in there?'

'The guinea-pigs ... And on the right are the typists' and clerks' offices.... We have other buildings at Pantin, from which most of the stuff is sent out, for you know of course that Dr Rivière's Serums are famous throughout the world....'

'Was it Couchet who put them on the market?'

'Yes! Dr Rivière had no money. Couchet financed his research. About ten years ago he set up a laboratory which wasn't on the scale of this one....'

'Is Dr Rivière still in the business?'

'He died five years ago in a motor accident.'

Couchet's body was taken away at last, and, when the door of the safe was opened, there were exclamations: all the money it contained had disappeared. Only business papers were left. Monsieur Philippe explained:

'There were not only the three hundred thousand francs that Monsieur Couchet must certainly have brought, but also sixty thousand francs that were paid in this morning, which I put in this pigeon-hole myself, with an elastic band round them!'

In the dead man's wallet, nothing! Or rather, two tickets

for a theatre near the Madeleine, at the sight of which Nine broke into sobs.

'They were for us!... We were to have gone there together!...'

Things were coming to an end. The confusion had increased. The photographers were folding up their ungainly camera-stands. The police doctor was washing his hands at a tap he had discovered in a closet and the examining magistrate's clerk was showing signs of weariness.

For a few moments, however, in spite of all this agitation, Maigret had a kind of *tête-à-tête* with the dead man.

He was a plump, sturdy, shortish man: like Nine, he had probably never shed a certain vulgarity, in spite of his well-cut suit, his manicured nails, his hand-made silk shirt and underclothes.

His fair hair was thinning. His eyes must have been blue, with a somewhat childish expression.

'A real good sort!' a voice sighed behind Maigret.

It was Nine, tearful with emotion, calling Maigret to witness since she dared not address the more forbidding Parquet people.

'I give you my word, he was a real good sort! As soon as he thought something would make me happy ... And not only me!... Anybody!... I never saw anyone tip the way he did.... So that I used to scold him.... I told him people took him for a sucker.... Then he used to say: "What does it matter?"'

The Inspector asked gravely:

'Was he usually cheerful?'

'Fairly cheerful.... But not deep down.... You understand?... It's hard to explain.... He always had to be moving about and doing something.... If he stayed still he grew gloomy or anxious....'

'His wife?...'

'I've seen her once in the distance. . . . I've nothing to say against her. . . .'

'Where did Couchet live?'

'Boulevard Haussmann. . . . But most of the time he went to Meulan, where he's got a villa. . . .'

Maigret glanced round sharply and saw the concierge, who, not daring to come in, was making signs to him, looking unhappier than ever.

'I say! . . . He's coming down. . . .'

'Who? . . .'

'Monsieur de Saint-Marc. . . . He must have heard all the noise. . . . Here he comes. . . . Today of all days! . . . Just think. . . .'

The former ambassador, who was in his dressing-gown, seemed reluctant to come forward. He had recognized a police visit. Besides, the corpse on its stretcher had just passed close to him.

'What has happened?' he asked Maigret.

'A man's been killed . . . Couchet, the owner of the Serum Laboratory. . . .'

The Inspector had the impression that his interlocutor had been struck by a sudden thought, as though he had remembered something.

'You knew him?'

'No . . . That's to say I've heard him spoken of. . . .'

'And? . . .'

'Nothing! I don't know anything. . . . At what time was . . . ?'

'The crime must have been committed between eight and nine o'clock. . . .'

Monsieur de Saint-Marc sighed, smoothed his silvery hair, nodded to Maigret, and went off towards the staircase that led to his own flat.

The concierge had remained on one side. Then she had gone to speak to someone who was walking to and fro in the entrance-way, head bent. When she came back towards the Inspector he questioned her.

'Who's that?'

'Monsieur Martin . . . He's looking for a glove he lost. . . . You see he never goes out without gloves, even to buy cigarettes over the way.'

Now, Monsieur Martin was prowling round the dustbins, striking a few matches, until at last he resignedly made his way upstairs again.

People were shaking hands with each other in the courtyard. The police were clearing out. The examining magistrate had a few words with Maigret.

'I'll leave you to your job. . . . Of course you'll keep me informed. . . .'

Monsieur Philippe, still as formal as a fashion plate, bowed to the Inspector.

'You don't need me any longer?'

'I'll see you tomorrow. . . . I suppose you'll be in your office? . . .'

'As usual. . . . At nine o'clock precisely. . . .'

And then there came a sudden moment of emotional tension, although not the slightest incident occurred. The courtyard was still immersed in shadow, save for its solitary lamp, the dusty bulb in the entrance.

Outside, the cars moved into gear and glided off over the asphalt, their headlamps for a moment lighting up the trees of the Place des Vosges.

The dead man was no longer there. The office seemed to have been ransacked. Nobody had thought of switching off the lights, and the laboratory was illuminated as though for intensive night work.

And here were the three of them together in the middle of the courtyard, three dissimilar beings who had not known one another an hour before and yet seemed bound together by some mysterious affinity.

Or rather, who were like the members of a family left behind, alone, after a funeral, when the outsiders have gone!

Such was the fleeting impression that struck Maigret as he looked, in turn, at Nine's piquant face and the haggard features of the concierge.

'You've put your children to bed?'

'Yes. . . . But they aren't asleep. . . . They're anxious . . . they seem to feel . . .'

Madame Bourcier had a question to ask, a question she seemed almost ashamed of and yet which, for her, was all-important.

'D'you think . . .'

Her eyes roamed round the courtyard and seemed to linger over the darkened windows.

'. . . that . . . that it's somebody from the house?'

And now she was staring at the entrance, at that broad porch whose door was always open – except after eleven at night – connecting the courtyard with the street, giving access to the building to all the unknown world outside.

Nine's attitude, meanwhile, was one of restraint, and from time to time she cast a furtive glance at the Inspector.

'The investigation will probably provide the answer to your question, Madame Bourcier. . . . For the time being, there's just one thing that seems certain; the person who stole the three hundred and sixty thousand francs is not the same as the murderer. . . . At least that's probable, since Monsieur Couchet had his back against the safe. . . . By the way, were the lights on in the laboratory this evening?'

'Wait a minute. . . . Yes, I believe so. . . . But not as much as now. . . . Monsieur Couchet must have switched on a light or two to go to the toilet, which is at the far end of the building. . . .'

Maigret went in to turn off all the lights, while the concierge stayed in the doorway even though the body was no longer there. In the courtyard the Inspector found Nine waiting for him. He heard a sound somewhere over his head, the sound of something brushing against a window pane.

But all the windows were shut, all the lights out.

Somebody had moved, somebody was keeping watch in a darkened room.

'I'll see you tomorrow, Madame Bourcier. . . . I shall be here before the offices open. . . .'

'I'm coming along with you! I've got to close the main door. . . .'

Outside on the pavement, Nine commented:

'I thought you had a car.'

She seemed unwilling to leave him. Her eyes fixed on the ground, she added:

'Whereabouts do you live?'

'Quite close by, Boulevard Richard-Lenoir.'

'The Métro's closed, I suppose?'

'I should think so.'

'I'd like to tell you something. . . .'

'I'm listening.'

She still dared not look at him. Behind them, they could hear the concierge bolting the door and then going back to her lodge. There was not a soul in the square. The fountains plashed musically. The town hall clock struck one.

'I know this must seem awful cheek. . . . I don't know what you'll think of me. . . . I told you Raymond was very generous. . . . He had no sense of the value of money. . . . He used to give me whatever I wanted. . . . You understand? . . .'

'And so?'

'It's ridiculous. . . . I used to ask for as little as possible. . . . I'd wait till it occurred to him. . . . Besides, as he was nearly always with me, I was never short of anything. . . .

'Tonight I was going to have dinner with him. . . . Well!
. . .'

'You're broke?'

'It's not exactly that!' she protested. 'It's even stupider!
I was going to have asked him for some money tonight. I
paid a bill at midday . . .'

She was in agonies. She was watching Maigret closely,
ready to draw back at the least hint of a smile.

'I'd never imagined he wouldn't come. . . . I still had a
little money in my bag. . . . While I was waiting for him at
the Select I ate some oysters, and then some crayfish. . . . I
telephoned. . . . And when I got here I realized I'd barely
got enough to pay my taxi. . . .'

'And at home?'

'I live in a hotel. . . .'

'I'm asking you whether you've got any money put
by. . . .'

'Me?'

A nervous little laugh.

'Whatever for? . . . Could I have known? . . . Even if I
had, I shouldn't have wanted . . .'

Maigret heaved a sigh.

'Come with me as far as Boulevard Beaumarchais. That's
the only place you'll find a taxi at this hour. What are you
going to do?'

'Nothing . . . I . . .'

All the same, a shiver ran through her. It's true that she
was only wearing a silk dress.

'Hadn't he made a will?'

'How should I know? . . . D'you think one worries about
things like that when everything's going well? . . . Raymond
was a real good sort . . . I . . .'

She was weeping silently as she walked. The Inspector
slipped a hundred-franc note into her hand, hailed a passing
cab, and grunted, thrusting his hands into his pockets:

'I'll see you tomorrow.... You did say Hôtel Pigalle?
...'

When he got into bed, Madame Maigret only woke up
enough to murmur half-consciously:

'I hope you've had some dinner?'

Chapter 3

The Couple in the
Hôtel Pigalle

When he left home at eight o'clock next morning Maigret
had three alternative tasks to choose from, all of which had
to be performed that day: to revisit the premises in the
Place des Vosges and question the staff; to pay a call
on Madame Couchet, who had been informed of events
by the local police; or, finally, to have another talk with
Nine.

As soon as he woke he had rung up Police Headquarters,
giving them a list of the tenants of the building and of
everyone who was closely or remotely connected with the
affair, and when he called in at his office he would find
detailed information awaiting him.

The market was in full swing on the Boulevard Richard-
Lenoir. It was so cold that the Inspector turned up the
velvet collar of his overcoat. The Place des Vosges was
close by, but he would have to go there on foot.

However, a tram was passing bound for the Place
Pigalle, and that decided Maigret's course of action. He
would see Nine first.

Of course, she wasn't up. At the hotel desk he was
recognized with some anxiety.

'She's not mixed up in anything tiresome, I hope? Such
a well-behaved girl!'

'Does she have many visitors?'

'Only her gentleman friend.'

'The old one or the young one?'

'She's only got one. Neither old nor young. . . .'

The hotel was a comfortable one, with a lift, and telephones in all the rooms. Maigret was deposited on the third floor, knocked at the door of number 27, and heard someone stirring in bed, then a voice mumble:

'What is it?'

'Open the door, Nine!'

A hand must have emerged from under the blankets and reached out to draw the bolt. Maigret entered the close, darkened room, caught sight of the young woman's piquant face, and went to draw the curtains.

'What time is it?'

'Not yet nine o'clock.... Don't disturb yourself....'

She was screwing up her eyes against the harsh daylight. Under such conditions she was not pretty, and she looked more like a little country girl than a coquette. She passed her hand over her face two or three times, and ended by sitting in the bed propped against the pillow. At last she unhooked the telephone.

'Bring my breakfast, please!'

And to Maigret:

'What a business!... You didn't mind my cadging from you last night, did you?... It's so silly!... I shall have to go and sell my jewellery....'

'Have you much?'

She pointed to the dressing table where, in an ashtray advertising somebody's goods, there lay a few rings, a bracelet, a watch, the whole lot worth about five thousand francs.

Somebody was knocking at the door of the neighbouring room, and Nine listened attentively; a faint smile crossed her lips when she heard the knocking renewed insistently.

'Who is it?' asked Maigret.

'Next door? I don't know! But if anyone's able to wake them up at this hour of the morning....'

'What d'you mean?'

'Nothing! They never get up before four in the afternoon, if then!'

'Do they take dope?'

Her eyelashes fluttered affirmatively, but she hurriedly added:

'You're not going to take advantage of my having told you, I hope?'

However, the door had eventually opened. So did Nine's, and a maid brought in a tray with *café au lait* and croissants.

'You'll excuse me?'

Her eyes were ringed, and her nightgown disclosed thin shoulders, and a small rather flaccid bosom like an undergrown schoolgirl's. While she dipped pieces of croissant into her coffee she went on listening as if, in spite of everything, she was interested in what was happening next door.

'Am I involved in the business?' she asked none the less. 'It would be tiresome if my name got into the papers! Especially for Madame Couchet....'

And as somebody was rapping a hasty low tattoo on the door, she called out:

'Come in!'

It was a woman of about thirty, who had slipped on a fur coat over her nightgown and whose feet were bare. She nearly beat a retreat on catching sight of Maigret's broad back, then she plucked up courage and stammered:

'I didn't know you had a visitor!'

The Inspector started when he heard that drawling voice, which seemed to issue with difficulty from a clogged mouth. He looked at the woman who was closing the door, and saw a colourless face with puffy eyelids. A quick glance from Nine confirmed his impression. This was undoubtedly the drug addict from next door.

'What's happened?'

'Nothing! Roger's got a visitor. So I've taken the liberty . . .'

She sat down at the foot of the bed, in a daze, and sighed as Nine had done:

'But what time is it?'

'Nine o'clock!' said Maigret. 'You look as if cocaine didn't suit you!'

'It's not cocaine. . . . It's ether. . . . Roger says that it's better and that . . .'

She was feeling cold. She moved to huddle over the radiator, and looked outside.

'It's going to rain again. . . .'

The whole scene was gloomy and despondent. There was a comb full of tangled hair on the dressing table. Nine's stockings were lying on the floor.

'I'm disturbing you, aren't I? But it's important, apparently. . . . It's about Roger's father, who's dead. . . .'

Maigret was looking at Nine and he noticed that she suddenly frowned as though some idea had struck her. At the same moment the woman who had just been speaking put her hand up to her chin reflectively, muttering to herself:

'Well, well!'

And the Inspector asked her:

'Did you know Roger's father?'

'I've never seen him. . . . But . . . wait a minute! . . . I say, Nine, nothing's happened to your friend, has it?'

Nine and the Inspector exchanged glances.

'Why?'

'I don't know. . . . I'm all in a muddle. . . . I suddenly thought how Roger told me one day that his father visited somebody in the hotel. . . . That amused him. . . . But he preferred not to meet him, and once when somebody was coming up the stairs he hurried back into the bedroom. . . . Now I've got the impression that this person came in here. . . .'

Nine had stopped eating. She seemed encumbered by the tray on her knees, and her face betrayed anxiety.

'His son?' she said slowly, her gaze fixed on the window, a rectangle of glaucous light.

'But then!...' the other woman exclaimed '... Then it's your friend who's dead!... Apparently it was murder....'

'Is Roger's name Couchet?' asked Maigret.

'Roger Couchet, yes!'

All three fell silent, ill at ease.

'What does he do?' the Inspector asked at last after a long pause, during which a murmur of voices could be heard from the neighbouring room.

'What d'you mean?'

'What's his profession?'

And the young woman suddenly retorted:

'You're police, aren't you?'

She was agitated. Perhaps she was about to blame Nine for having led her into a trap.

'The Inspector's very kind,' said Nine, putting one leg out of her bed and leaning over to pick up her stockings.

'I might have guessed it!... But then you already knew before ... before I came....'

'I had never heard of Roger!' said Maigret. 'Now you'll have to tell me a few things about him....'

'I don't know anything.... We've only been together about three weeks....'

'And before that?'

'He was with a tall redhead who calls herself a manicurist....'

'Does he work?'

That word was enough to make her embarrassment more obvious.

'I don't know....'

'In other words, he does nothing.... Is he well off? Does he spend his money freely?'

'No! We almost always eat at a cheap *prix-fixe* restaurant ... six francs. ...'

'Does he often talk about his father?'

'He only mentioned him once to me, as I told you. ...'

'Will you tell me about the person who's visiting him now? Had you met him before?'

'No! It's a man ... well, I don't know how to describe him. I took him for a process-server and when I came in here, I thought that was it, and that Roger was in debt. ...'

'Is he well dressed?'

'Well ... I saw a bowler hat, a fawn overcoat, gloves. ...'

There was a connecting door between the two rooms hidden by a curtain, and probably sealed up. Maigret could have put his ear to it and overheard everything, but he was reluctant to do so in front of the two women.

Nine got dressed: the only toilet she managed was dabbing her face with a wet cloth. She was on edge; her movements were jerky. Clearly, things had got beyond her, and she was expecting unrelieved disaster, lacking the strength to react, or even to try and understand.

The other was calmer, perhaps because she was still under the influence of ether, perhaps because she had more experience of this sort of thing.

'What's your name?'

'Céline.'

'Have you a job?'

'I used to be a visiting hairdresser.'

'Is your name on the Vice Squad's list?'

She shook her head, without indignation. And the mutter of voices could still be heard next door.

Nine, who had slipped on a dress, was looking round the room, and all of a sudden burst into tears, stammering:

'Oh God, oh God!'

'It's a queer business,' Céline said slowly. 'And if there's really been a crime, we're going to be in a mess. ...'

'Where were you at eight o'clock last night?'

She pondered. 'Wait a minute.... Eight o'clock....
Why, I was at the Cyrano....'

'Was Roger with you?'

'No.... We really can't be together the whole time.... I
met him again at midnight at the *tabac* in the rue Fontaine....'

'Did he tell you where he'd been?'

'I didn't ask him....'

Through the window Maigret could see the Place
Pigalle, its tiny garden, the hoardings advertising night-
clubs. Then suddenly he stood up and walked towards the
door.

'Wait for me, both of you!'

And he went out, knocked at the neighbouring door and,
without waiting, turned its handle.

A man in pyjamas was sitting in the only armchair in the
room, which, in spite of the open window, was pervaded by
a sickly smell of ether. Another man was walking about,
gesticulating. It was Monsieur Martin, whom Maigret had
met twice the night before, in the courtyard in the Place des
Vosges.

'Well, so you've found your glove!'

And Maigret scrutinized the hands of the official
from Wills and Probate, who turned so pale that the
Inspector thought for one moment that he was going
to faint. His lips were trembling. He tried in vain to
speak.

'I ... I ...'

The young man in the chair was unshaven. His face was
waxen, his eyes red-rimmed, his loose lips betrayed his weak
character. He was greedily drinking water from the tooth-
glass.

'Calm down, Monsieur Martin! I hadn't expected to find

you here, particularly at an hour when your office must have been open long ago.'

He was looking the fellow over from head to foot. He had to make an effort not to feel sorry for him, the wretched man seemed in such distress.

From his shoes to his tie, fixed to a celluloid collar, Monsieur Martin was the caricaturists' prototype of the petty official. A neat, respectable functionary with well-waxed moustaches, not a speck of dust on his clothes, who would undoubtedly think it below his dignity to go out without gloves on his hands.

Now he didn't know what to do with those hands, and his eyes roamed round the untidy room as if in search of inspiration.

'May I ask you one question, Monsieur Martin? How long have you known Roger Couchet?'

Instead of terror, the man now displayed bewilderment.

'Me?'

'Yes, you!'

'Why, since . . . ever since my marriage!'

He said this as if the thing was self-evident.

'I don't follow!'

'Roger is my stepson. . . . The son of my wife. . . .'

'And of Raymond Couchet?'

'Why, yes. . . . Because . . .'

He was recovering his self-possession.

'My wife was Couchet's first wife. . . . They had one son, Roger. . . . When she got her divorce, I married her. . . .'

The effect of this was as if a squall of wind had cleared the sky of clouds. The house in the Place des Vosges was completely transformed. The character of events was changed. Certain points became clearer. Others, on the other hand, became more obscure, more disturbing.

So much so that Maigret dared not say anything more.

He felt the need to get his thoughts straight. He looked in turn at the two men with growing uneasiness.

Only the night before, staring up at all the windows visible from the courtyard, the concierge had asked him:

'D'you think it was somebody from the house?'

And her gaze had finally come to rest on the entrance. She hoped that the murderer had come in that way, somebody from outside.

Well, it wasn't so! The drama concerned the inhabitants of the house! Maigret was quite unable to say why, but he was sure of it.

But what sort of drama? That he didn't know!

Only he felt that invisible threads were stretching out, connecting such very different points in space, going from the Place des Vosges to this hotel in the rue Pigalle, from the Martins' flat to the office at the Rivière Serums laboratory, from Nine's bedroom to that of the ether-doped couple.

The most disturbing thing, perhaps, was to see Monsieur Martin flung like an unconscious spinning-top into this labyrinth. He was still wearing gloves. His buff overcoat in itself implied a respectable and orderly existence. And his uneasy gaze was trying to settle somewhere, without success.

'I came to tell Roger . . .' he stammered.

'Yes?'

Maigret looked him in the eyes, calmly and penetratingly, and he almost expected to see his interlocutor shrivel up with anguish.

'My wife suggested, you see, that it would be better if we should . . .'

'I understand!'

'Roger is very . . .'

'Very sensitive!' Maigret finished off. 'A highly-strung creature!'

The young man, who was now drinking his third glass of water, glared at him resentfully. He must have been about twenty-five, but his features were already worn, his eyelids withered.

He was still handsome, nevertheless, with the sort of good looks that some women find irresistible. His skin was smooth, and even his weary, somewhat disillusioned expression had a certain romantic quality.

'Tell me, Roger Couchet, did you often see your father?'

'From time to time!'

'Where?' And Maigret looked at him sternly.

'In his office. . . . Or else at a restaurant. . . .'

'When did you see him last?'

'I don't know. . . . Some weeks ago. . . .'

'And you asked him for money?'

'As usual!'

'In short, you sponged on him?'

'He was rich enough to. . . .'

'One minute! Where were you yesterday evening about eight o'clock?'

There was no shadow of hesitation.

'At the Select!' he said with an ironical smile which implied: 'If you think I can't see what you're getting at!'

'What were you doing at the Select?'

'Waiting for my father!'

'So you needed money! And you knew he would come to the Select. . . .'

'He was there almost every evening with his tart! Besides, that afternoon I'd heard him speak over the telephone. . . . For you can hear everything that's being said next door . . .'

'When you saw that your father wasn't coming, it didn't occur to you to visit his office in the Place des Vosges?'

'No!'

From the mantelpiece Maigret picked up a photograph of

the young man, which stood there surrounded by numerous feminine portraits. He thrust it into his pocket, muttering:

'If you'll allow me!'

'Just as you please!'

'You surely don't believe ...' began Monsieur Martin.

'I don't believe anything at all. That reminds me to ask you a few questions. What sort of relations did you and your wife have with Roger?'

'He didn't often visit us.'

'And when he did?'

'He only stayed a few minutes....'

'Does his mother know the sort of life he leads?'

'What d'you mean?'

'Don't play the simpleton, Monsieur Martin! Does your wife know that her son lives in Montmartre, doing nothing?'

And the civil servant stared at the floor, uneasily.

'I often tried to get him to take a job!' he sighed.

This time the young man began drumming on the table impatiently.

'I'd like to point out that I'm still in my pyjamas, and that ...'

'Will you tell me if you saw anybody you knew at the Select last night?'

'I saw Nine!'

'Did you speak to her?'

'If you don't mind! I've never addressed a word to her!'

'Where was she sitting?'

'At the second table to the right of the bar.'

'Where did you find your glove, Monsieur Martin? If I remember rightly, you were hunting for it last night around the dustbins in the courtyard....'

Monsieur Martin uttered a strained little laugh.

'It was at home! ... Just imagine, I'd gone out with one glove on and I hadn't noticed....'

'When you left the Place des Vosges where did you go?'

'I went for a walk. . . . Along the embankment . . . I . . . I had a headache. . . .'

'Do you often go for walks in the evening without your wife?'

'Sometimes!'

He was in agonies. And he still did not know what to do with his gloved hands.

'Are you going to your office now?'

'No! I telephoned to ask for the day off. I can't leave my wife in . . .'

'Well, go back to her now!'

Maigret stood there. The poor fellow was searching for some way of taking his leave decently.

'Good-bye, Roger. . . .' he gulped. 'I . . . I think you ought to see your mother. . . .'

But Roger merely shrugged his shoulders and stared impatiently at Maigret. The sound of Monsieur Martin's footsteps died away down the stairs.

The young man said nothing. His hand automatically took hold of a flask of ether on the bedside table and set it down further off.

'You've no statement to make?' the Inspector asked him slowly.

'None!'

'Because, if you had anything to say, it would be better to do so now than later. . . .'

'I shan't have anything to tell you later. . . . Yes! One thing, which I'll say right away: you're making a hell of a big mistake. . . .'

'By the way, since you didn't see your father last night you must be out of money?'

'You've said it!'

'Where are you going to find any?'

'Don't worry about me, please. . . . Now, if you'll excuse

me. . . .' And he poured some water into the basin to begin his toilet.

Maigret, for form's sake, took a few more steps round the room, then left it and went next door, where the two women were waiting for him. Céline was now the more agitated of the two. As for Nine, she was sitting in the easy-chair, slowly gnawing at her handkerchief as her great dreamy eyes stared out of the window at nothing.

'Well?' inquired Roger's mistress.

'Nothing! You can go back now. . . .'

'Was it really his father who? . . .'

And suddenly growing grave, with furrowed brow:

'But in that case he'll inherit?'

And she went off, deep in thought.

On the pavement, Maigret asked his companion:

'Where are you going?'

A vague, apathetic gesture, then:

'I'm going to the Moulin Bleu to see if they'll have me back. . . .'

He watched her with affectionate interest.

'Were you very fond of Couchet?'

'I told you yesterday: he was a real good sort – and there aren't so many of them about I can tell you! When you think that some swine has . . .'

Two tears welled up, and that was all.

'Here we are!' she said, opening a little side door which was the artists' entrance.

Maigret, who was thirsty, went into a bar and ordered a half pint. He had to go to the Place des Vosges. The sight of a telephone reminded him that he had not yet looked in at the Quai des Orfèvres, where urgent mail might be awaiting him.

He rang up the office boy.

'Is that you, Jean? ... Anything for me? ... What's

that? . . . A lady been waiting for an hour? . . . In mourning? . . . Not Madame Couchet? . . . What d'you say? . . . Madame Martin? . . . I'm coming right away!'

Madame Martin *in mourning*! And she'd been waiting for him for an hour in the waiting-room at Police Headquarters!

Maigret knew her only as a shadow: the curious shadow seen the night before, against the curtain of a second-floor window, when she was gesticulating and moving her lips excitedly to utter terrible diatribes.

'It often happens!' the concierge had said.

And the poor little fellow from the Wills and Probate Office, who had forgotten his glove, had gone off for a walk by himself in the darkness of the riverside. . . .

And when Maigret had left the courtyard, at one in the morning, there had been the sound of something brushing against a window pane!

He went slowly up the dusty staircase of Police Headquarters, shaking hands with a few colleagues on the way, and put his head through the half-open door of the waiting-room.

Ten armchairs, upholstered in green velvet. A sort of billiard table. On the wall, the roll of honour: two hundred portraits of detectives killed in the performance of their duty.

In the middle armchair, a woman in black sat very stiffly, one hand holding a handbag with a silver clasp, the other resting on the handle of an umbrella.

Thin lips. A determined gaze fixed straight ahead.

She did not flinch when she felt herself being watched.

With set features, she waited.

Chapter 4

The Second-Floor Window

She walked ahead of Maigret with the aggressive dignity of those for whom someone else's irony is the worst of disasters.

'Please sit down, madame!'

It was a clumsy, good-natured, dreamy-eyed Maigret who ushered her in and motioned her to a chair directly under the pallid square of light from the window. She sat down in it, assuming exactly the same attitude as in the waiting-room.

A dignified attitude, evidently! And also a militant one. Her shoulders did not touch the chair-back. And the hand in its black cotton glove was ready to gesticulate without dropping the handbag, which would swing about in the air.

'I suppose, Inspector, you must be wondering why I . . .'

'No!'

It was not out of unkindness that Maigret chose to disconcert her in this way on their first contact. Neither was it by chance. He knew it was necessary.

He himself sat in an office armchair. He was leaning back in a somewhat vulgar attitude and smoking his pipe in greedy little puffs.

Madame Martin had given a start, or rather her shoulders had stiffened.

'What do you mean? I fancy you were not expecting . . .'

'Yes!'

And he gave her a bland smile. This time, her fingers

seemed uneasy in their black cotton gloves. Her piercing eyes scanned the horizon, and suddenly Madame Martin had an inspiration.

'You've had an anonymous letter?'

Her question was a statement, made with a forced air of being certain of what she was suggesting, which made the Inspector's smile even broader, for this too was a characteristic trait which fitted in with all he had already learnt about the lady.

'I've had no anonymous letter. . . .'

She shook her head sceptically.

'You're not going to make me believe . . .'

She seemed to have stepped straight out of a family photograph album. Physically, she was a perfect match for the civil servant she had married.

It was easy to imagine them, for instance, walking up the Champs-Élysées on a Sunday afternoon: Madame Martin's wiry, black-clad back, her hat always askew on account of her chignon, her busy, hurried walk, and that jerk of the chin underlining categorical remarks. . . . And Martin's buff overcoat, his leather gloves, his stick, his steady, peaceful way of walking, his attempts to linger and pause in front of shop windows. . . .

'Had you got mourning clothes at home?' Maigret murmured insidiously, blowing out a big puff of smoke.

'My sister died three years ago . . . I mean my sister at Blois, the one who married a police inspector. . . . You see that . . .'

'That what? . . .'

Nothing! She'd been warning him! It was time to make him feel that she wasn't just anybody!

Moreover she was growing nervous, because the whole of the speech she had prepared was useless, thanks to this stupid Inspector.

'When did you hear about your first husband's death?'

'Why ... this morning, like everybody else! It was the concierge who told me you were in charge of the case and, as my position is somewhat delicate. . . . You can't possibly understand.'

'Oh yes, I can! By the way, didn't your son pay you a visit yesterday afternoon?'

'What are you trying to insinuate?'

'Nothing! A simple question.'

'The concierge will tell you that it's at least three weeks since he came to see me. . . .'

She was speaking drily. Her expression was more aggressive. Had Maigret been wrong not to let her make her speech?

'I'm very glad of your visit, for it proves your conscientiousness and . . .'

At the mere word *conscientiousness* something altered in the woman's grey eyes, and she thanked him with a nod.

'Certain situations are so painful!' she said. 'Many people don't understand. Even my husband, who advised me not to wear mourning! Note that I'm not really in deep mourning. No veil, no crêpe! Just black clothes. . . .'

He signified approval with a jerk of his chin, and laid his pipe on the table.

'Even though we were divorced and Roger has made me unhappy, I couldn't . . .'

She was recovering her self-assurance. Almost imperceptibly, she was getting back to her prepared speech.

'Particularly in a big house like ours, where there are twenty-eight families! And what families! I'm not referring to the first-floor tenants. Although even they! . . . Monsieur de Saint-Marc is a gentleman, but as for his wife, *she* wouldn't say good morning to you for all the money in the world. . . . When one's been carefully brought up, it's painful to . . .'

'Were you born in Paris?'

'My father was a confectioner in Meaux.'

'How old were you when you married Couchet?'

'I was twenty. . . . Of course my parents never let me serve in the shop. . . . In those days Couchet was a traveller. . . . He said he was making plenty of money and would be able to give a woman what she wanted. . . .'

Her eyes hardened, guarding against any hint of irony in Maigret's expression.

'I'd rather not speak of what I went through with him! . . . Whatever money he made he frittered away on absurd projects. . . . He claimed he was going to get rich. . . . He changed his job three times a year, so that when my son was born we hadn't a penny saved and my mother had to pay for the baby's layette. . . .'

She had put down her umbrella at last, leaning it against the desk. Maigret reflected that she must have been speaking with the same curt vehemence the night before, when he had noticed her shadow outlined against the curtain.

'When a man's incapable of providing for a woman he has no right to get married! That's what I maintain! And particularly when he has no pride! For I hardly dare mention all the jobs that Couchet did. . . . I used to tell him to look for a respectable situation, something that would bring in a pension. . . . In the Civil Service, for instance! . . . At any rate, if anything had happened to him then I'd not have been left destitute. . . . Not him! He even went so far as to trail around with the cyclists' Tour de France in some capacity or other. . . . He'd go on ahead and see to supplies, or something of the sort! And he'd come back without a penny! . . . That was the kind of man he was! And that was the life I led. . . .'

'Where did you live?'

'At Nanterre! For we couldn't even afford a place in town. . . . Did you know Couchet? . . . He didn't mind!

44

He had no sense of shame! He never worried! He maintained that he was born to make a lot of money and that he would make it. . . . After bicycles, it was watch-chains. . . . No, you'll never guess! Watch-chains that he sold at a booth in a fair, Inspector! And my sisters dared not visit the fair at Neuilly for fear of seeing him there! . . .'

'It was you who asked for a divorce?'

She dropped her eyes modestly, but her features remained tense.

'Monsieur Martin lived in the same building as we did. . . . He was younger than he is now. . . . He had a good post in the Civil Service. . . . Couchet was always leaving me alone and gadding about to try his luck. . . . Oh, it was all perfectly respectable! . . . . I told my husband what I thought of him. . . . Divorce was by mutual consent, for incompatibility of temperament. . . . Couchet merely had to pay me an allowance for the boy. . . .

'And we waited a year, Martin and I, before getting married. . . .'

Now she was wriggling on her chair. Her fingers were twitching at the silver clasp of her handbag.

'I tell you, I've never had any luck. To begin with, Couchet didn't even pay the allowance regularly! And it's painful for a sensitive woman to see her second husband paying for the upkeep of a child that's not his own. . . .'

No! Maigret was not asleep, even though his eyes were half closed and the pipe between his teeth had gone out.

It was getting more painful. The woman's eyes were filling with tears. Her lips began to quiver distressingly.

'Nobody but myself knows what I suffered. . . . I sent Roger to school . . . I wanted to give him a good education. . . . He wasn't like his father. . . . He was affectionate and sensitive. . . . When he was seventeen Martin found him a place in a bank, to learn the job. . . . But that was when he ran into Couchet somewhere or other. . . .'

'And he got into the habit of asking his father for money?'

'I'll have you know that Couchet had always refused me everything! Everything cost too much for me! I used to make my own dresses and wear the same hat three years running. ...'

'And he gave Roger whatever he wanted?'

'He completely spoiled him! ... Roger left home and went to live on his own. ... He still comes to visit me from time to time. ... But he used to go and see his father too! ...'

'How long have you been living in the Place des Vosges?'

'About eight years. ... When we found the flat we didn't even know that Couchet was in the serum business. ... Martin wanted to leave. ... That would have been the last straw! ... If somebody had to go it should have been Couchet, surely! ... Couchet who'd got rich, goodness knows how, and who used to turn up in a car driven by a chauffeur! ... For he'd even got a chauffeur. ... I've seen his wife. ...'

'At her own home?'

'I watched for her on the pavement, to find out what she was like. ... I'd rather not give my opinion. ... Nothing so very wonderful, in any case, in spite of the airs she puts on and her Astrakhan coat. ...'

Maigret passed a hand across his forehead. This was turning into a nightmare. For a quarter of an hour he had been staring at the same face and he felt as if he would never get it out of his mind's eye.

A thin, faded face, with delicate mobile features, which must never have expressed anything but pained resignation.

And this again put him in mind of certain family portraits, indeed of members of his own family. He'd had an aunt, stouter than Madame Martin but, like her, given to incessant lamentation. Whenever she came to Maigret's home in his childhood, he knew that as soon as she sat down she would pull a handkerchief from her bag.

'My poor dear Hermance! . . .' she would begin. 'What a life! I must tell you the latest thing Pierre has done. . . .'

And she had the same mobile features, the same excessively thin lips, the same wild glint in her eyes.

Madame Martin had suddenly lost the thread of her ideas. She was growing excited.

'Now you must understand my position. . . . Of course, Couchet married again. All the same I was his wife, I was with him at the beginning of his career, that's to say all through the hardest years of his life. . . . The other woman's a mere doll. . . .'

'You intend to claim the inheritance?'

'Me? . . .' she exclaimed indignantly. 'I wouldn't have his money for anything in the world! We're not wealthy! Martin's got no initiative, he doesn't know how to put himself forward, he lets less intelligent colleagues cut the ground from under his feet. . . . But even if it meant I had to go charring for a living I'd never consent. . . .'

'Did you send your husband to tell Roger?'

She did not turn any paler, for this would scarcely have been possible. The uniform grey of her complexion remained unchanged. But her glance wavered.

'How do you know?'

And in sudden indignation:

'I hope we're not being followed? Look here! . . . That would be the limit! . . . And if that's the case I'd have no hesitation about making a complaint to the authorities. . . .'

'Keep calm, madame. . . . I didn't say anything of the sort. . . . It was purely by chance that I met Monsieur Martin this morning. . . .'

But she was still suspicious, keeping hostile watch on the Inspector.

'I shall end by being sorry I came! . . . One tries to do the right thing! . . . And instead of being grateful . . .'

'I assure you I'm extremely grateful to you for coming. . . .'

She felt none the less that something had gone wrong. She was afraid of this big, broad-shouldered, bull-necked man, who was staring at her with such innocent, uncalculating eyes.

'In any case,' she declared in sharp, emphatic tones, 'it's better you should hear it from me than from the concierge. . . . And you'd have found out eventually. . . .'

'That you are the first Madame Couchet. . . .'

'Have you seen the other?'

Maigret found it hard to suppress a smile.

'Not yet. . . .'

'Oh, she'll shed some crocodile tears. . . . All the same she's well off now, with all the millions Couchet's made. . . .'

And then suddenly she was in tears, her lower lip was quivering, and this transformed her face, taking away its excessive sharpness.

'She didn't even know him when he was struggling, when he needed a woman to help and encourage him. . . .'

From time to time a muffled sob, barely perceptible, broke out in the stringy throat encircled by a band of *moiré* silk.

She rose. She looked round her to make sure she had forgotten nothing. She was sniffling.

'But all that doesn't count. . . .'

A bitter smile, beneath her tears.

'In any case I've done my duty. . . . I don't know what you think of me, but . . .'

'I assure you that . . .'

He would have found it difficult to complete his sentence if she had not gone on herself:

'I don't care! My conscience is clear! Not everybody can say as much!'

She felt something was missing. She did not know what. She glanced round the room again, and waved one hand, as though surprised to find it empty.

Maigret stood up and showed her to the door.

'Thank you for coming as you did. . . .'

'I acted as I thought right. . . .'

She was out in the passage, where a group of detectives were chatting and laughing. She walked past them with great dignity, without turning her head.

And Maigret, closing the door again, walked to the window and flung it open, in spite of the cold. He felt exhausted, as though after the strenuous cross-examination of some criminal. Above all he was conscious of that indefinable discomfort one feels on looking at certain aspects of life which one usually prefers to ignore.

There was nothing dramatic about it, nothing disgusting.

She had said nothing out of the ordinary. She had revealed nothing sensational to the Inspector.

And yet his interview with her left him with a feeling of nausea.

On a corner of the desk the police journal was open, showing the photographs of a score of 'Wanted' criminals. Brutish faces for the most part, heads bearing all the marks of degeneracy.

Ernst Strowitz, sentenced in absentia *by the Court of Caen for the murder of a farmer's wife on the Benouville road . . .*'

And a comment in red letters: *Dangerous. Always carries arms.*

A fellow who would fight ruthlessly for his life. Well, Maigret would rather have to deal with him than with all this slimy greyness, these family quarrels, and the crime which was still inexplicable, but whose haunting horror he could guess at.

A vision obsessed him: the Martins, as he pictured them walking down the Champs-Élysées on a Sunday. The buff overcoat and the black silk ribbon round the woman's neck. . . .

He rang. Jean appeared and Maigret sent him to fetch the files he had asked for about everyone connected with the drama.

There was nothing much. Nine had been arrested once and once only, in Montmartre, during a raid, and she had been released on proving that she did not live by prostitution.

As for young Couchet, he was being watched by the squad in charge of gambling establishments and by the men of the 'Society' branch, who suspected him of being involved in drug trafficking. But nothing definite had ever been pinned on him.

A telephone call to the Vice Squad. Céline, whose surname was Loiseau and who was born at Saint-Amand-Montrond, was well known there. She had her card. She came fairly regularly for inspection.

'She's not a bad girl!' the sergeant said. 'She usually sticks to one or two regular boyfriends. It's only when she falls back on street-walking again that we pick her up. . . .'

Jean, the office boy, was still in the room, and he pointed out something to Maigret.

'That lady forgot her umbrella. . . .'

'I know. . . .'

'Oh!'

'Yes, I need it.'

And the inspector got up with a sigh, went to close the window, and then stood with his back to the fire in the attitude he usually took up when he needed to think.

An hour later, he was able to make a mental summary of

the notes that had reached him from the various departments, and which were spread out on his desk.

In the first place, the autopsy report confirming the police doctor's theory: the shot had been fired from less than three yards and death had been instantaneous. The dead man's stomach contained a small quantity of alcohol, but no solid food.

The photographers from the Technical Branch, who worked in the basement of the Palais de Justice, declared that no interesting fingerprints had been picked up.

Finally the Crédit Lyonnais stated that Couchet, who was well known there, had visited the company's registered offices at about half past three and taken away three hundred thousand francs in new notes, as was his custom at the end of the month, before pay-day.

It was thus fairly well established that when he reached the Place des Vosges Couchet had deposited the three hundred thousand francs in the safe, beside the sixty thousand which were already there.

As he still had some work to do he had not closed the safe, which he was leaning against.

The light in the laboratory suggested that at a certain moment he had left the office, either to inspect some other part of the premises or, as was more likely, to visit the toilet.

Was the money still in the safe when he returned to his seat?

Presumably not, for in that case the murderer would have been obliged to push the body to one side in order to pull open the heavy door and get hold of the notes.

This was the technical aspect of the matter. Was the thief a murderer, or had a thief and a murderer acted separately?

Maigret paid a ten minute call on the examining magistrate to pass on the results so far obtained. Then, as it was a little after noon, he went home, hunching his back, always a sign of ill humour.

'Are you in charge of this Place des Vosges case?' inquired his wife, who had read the newspaper.

'I am!'

And Maigret sat down and looked at his wife in an odd way, in which increased tenderness was mingled with a hint of anxiety.

He could still visualize the thin face, the black garments, the anguished eyes of Madame Martin.

And those tears that had suddenly gushed forth, disappeared as though dried up by some inner fire, and broken out again a little later!

Madame Couchet with her furs, Madame Martin with none ... Couchet, supplying provisions for the cyclists in the Tour de France, and his first wife wearing the same hat three years running....

And their son.... And the flask of ether on the bedside table in the Hôtel Pigalle....

And Céline, who only took up street-walking when she was temporarily without a steady boyfriend....

And Nine....

'You don't look happy.... You look ill.... Perhaps you're sickening for a cold.'

It was quite true! Maigret felt a tickling in his nostrils and a sort of emptiness in his head.

'Whatever's that umbrella you've brought back? It's hideous! ...'

Madame Martin's umbrella! The Martin couple, buff overcoat and black silk dress, parading down the Champs-Élysées on a Sunday! ...

'It's nothing.... I don't know what time I'll be back!'

It was one of those impressions one cannot explain: there seemed to be something abnormal about the house, something that was recognizable even from the outside.

The excited bustle in the shop that sold beaded funeral wreaths? Evidently the tenants must have clubbed together to send a wreath.

The anxious glances cast by the ladies' hairdresser whose shop stood open on the other side of the entrance?

In any case, there was an unhealthy atmosphere about the house that day. And as it was four o'clock and darkness was beginning to fall, the absurd little lamp was already glowing under the archway.

Over the way, the keeper of the square garden was closing the gates. On the first floor, the Saint-Marcs' manservant was drawing the curtains, slowly and conscientiously.

When Maigret knocked at the door of the lodge, he found Madame Bourcier, the concierge, relating the whole story to an errand-boy from Dufayel's who carried a little inkpot slung across his blue uniform.

'A house where nothing's ever happened. . . . Hush, here's the Inspector. . . .'

She bore a vague resemblance to Madame Martin, in that both women seemed of indefinite age and indeed sexless. And both had been unhappy, or had thought themselves unhappy.

But the concierge also wore a look of resignation, a resignation to her lot that was almost like an animal's.

'Jojo . . . Lili. . . . Don't get in the way. . . . Good afternoon, Inspector . . . I'd expected you this morning. . . . What a business! . . . I hope I did right in sending round a subscription list for a wreath to all the tenants. . . . Is it known when the funeral's to be? . . . By the way . . . Madame de Saint-Marc . . . You know! . . . I must ask you not to say anything to her about it. . . . Monsieur de Saint-Marc came this morning. . . . He's afraid of upsetting her, in her present condition. . . .'

In the blue haze of the courtyard, the two lamps, the

one in the entrance and the one fastened to the wall, cast long shafts of yellowish light.

'Madame Martin's flat?' inquired Maigret.

'Second floor, third door on your left after you've turned the corner.'

The Inspector recognized the window, where the light was on but where no shadow could be seen against the curtain.

The rattle of typewriters could be heard from down by the laboratories. A delivery man appeared:

'Dr Rivière's Serums?'

'At the far end of the courtyard, on your right! Will you leave your sister alone, Jojo!'

Maigret made his way up the staircase, with Madame Martin's umbrella under his arm. As far as the first floor, the house had been redecorated, the walls were freshly painted and the staircase varnished.

On reaching the second floor one was in a different world, with dirty walls and worn floorboards. The doors of the apartments were painted an ugly brown, and fastened on these doors were either visiting cards or small plaques of embossed aluminium.

A cheap visiting card read: *Monsieur and Madame Edgar Martin.* To the right hung a tricolour twisted cord ending in a limp tassel. When Maigret pulled it, a shrill bell rang in the empty-sounding apartment. Then there were rapid steps. A voice asked:

'Who is there?'

'I've brought back your umbrella.'

The door opened. The hall consisted of a space a yard square where the buff overcoat hung on a coat-stand. Opposite, an open door revealed a room that was part dining-room, part drawing-room, with a radio set on a sideboard.

'I apologize for bothering you. This morning you forgot this umbrella in my office. . . .'

'You see! And I thought I'd left it on the bus. As I said to Martin . . .'

Maigret did not smile. He was used to the sort of women who insist on calling their husbands by their surnames.

Martin was there, wearing a smoking jacket of heavy chocolate-brown cloth over his striped trousers.

'Please come in. . . .'

'I don't want to disturb you. . . .'

'People who have nothing to hide never mind being disturbed!'

The essential characteristic of any dwelling is probably its smell. Here, it was a faint pervasive aroma of polish, cooking, and old clothes.

A canary was hopping about in a cage and occasionally spilling a drop of water.

'Give the Inspector the armchair!'

The armchair! There was just the one, a tall chair upholstered in such dark leather that it looked almost black.

And Madame Martin, very different to what she had been that morning, was simpering:

'You'll surely take something . . . I insist! . . . Martin! Bring an apéritif. . . .'

Martin looked worried. Perhaps there was none in the house? Perhaps only a drop at the bottom of the bottle?

'No, thank you, madame! I never drink before meals.'

'But you've plenty of time. . . .'

It was depressing! Depressing enough to make one discouraged with being a man, with living in a world where, after all, the sun shines several hours a day and real birds fly about freely!

These people couldn't have been fond of light, for the three electric lamps were carefully veiled by thick coloured shades which let only the bare minimum of light filter through.

'And above all, polish!' thought Maigret.

For that was what predominated in the smell! Moreover, the massive oak table gleamed like a skating rink.

Monsieur Martin had assumed the formal smile of a host.

'You must have a marvellous view over the Place des Vosges, which is something unique in Paris!' said Maigret, knowing perfectly well that the windows overlooked the courtyard.

'No! The rooms at the front on the second floor have got very low ceilings because of the style of the building. ... You know the whole square is scheduled as a historic monument. ... Nobody's entitled to make any alterations. ... And it's deplorable. ... For years now we've wanted to put in a bathroom and ...'

Maigret had gone up to the window. With a careless gesture he drew aside the blind on which he had seen the silhouette. And he stood there quite still, so excited that he forgot to make polite conversation.

Facing him were the offices and laboratory of Couchet's firm.

From below, he had noticed that the windows were of frosted glass.

From up here, he discovered that these were only the lower windows. The others were clear and transparent, washed two or three times a week by charwomen.

And in the very place where Couchet had been killed, he could distinctly see Monsieur Philippe signing the typed letters that his secretary passed him one by one. He could make out the lock of the safe.

And the communicating door into the laboratory was ajar. Through the windows of the latter a row of women in white overalls could be seen at a long table, busily packing up glass tubes.

Each had her job. The first picked the unwrapped tubes out of a basket and the ninth handed over to an assistant perfect parcels, neatly wrapped and labelled, all ready to be delivered to the chemists' shops.

'Aren't you going to bring some drinks?' Madame Martin's voice sounded behind Maigret. And her husband bustled about, opened a cupboard, clattered glasses.

'Just a tiny drop of vermouth, Inspector! ... Madame Couchet, of course, could undoubtedly offer you cock-tails....'

And Madame Martin's smile was as venomous as if her lips had been poisoned arrows.

Chapter 5

The Madwoman

Glass in hand, Maigret remarked, with his eye on Madame Martin:

'Well, if only you'd been looking through the window last night! My investigation would have been over by now! For you can't help seeing everything that goes on in Couchet's office from here.'

There was nothing meaningful about his voice or attitude. He was merely making small talk as he sipped his vermouth.

'I might even say that this case would have been of quite exceptional interest, from the point of view of evidence. Somebody actually witnessing the murder from a distance! Indeed, with field-glasses, one could see people's lips so clearly that one could piece together their conversation. . . .'

Madame Martin was at a loss, keeping on her guard, with her pale lips set in a noncommittal smile.

'But what an emotional experience for you! To be sitting quietly at your window, and suddenly to see somebody threatening your former husband! Worse still, for the scene must have been more complex. I imagine Couchet all alone, deep in his accounts. . . . He gets up and goes towards the toilet. When he comes back somebody has been rifling the safe, and hasn't had time to escape. . . . Nevertheless, there's one curious detail, in this case: that Couchet should have sat down again. . . . Of course, he may have known the thief? . . . He speaks to him. . . . He reproaches him, asks him to give back the money. . . .'

'Only I'd have had to be at the window!' commented Madame Martin.

'Perhaps other windows on the same floor have the same view? ... Who lives on your right?'

'Two girls and their mother.... The ones who play the gramophone every night....'

At that moment a cry rang out, a cry that Maigret had heard before. He stood silent for a moment, and then said softly:

'It's the madwoman, isn't it?'

'Hush....' said Madame Martin, moving noiselessly towards the door.

She opened it suddenly. In the dimly lit passage a woman's figure could be seen, hastily retreating.

'The old witch!...' muttered Madame Martin loud enough to be heard by the other woman.

Retracing her steps in a rage, she explained to the Inspector:

'That was old Mathilde! She used to be a cook! Have you seen her? She looks like a great toad! She lives in the next room with her sister, who's crazy. And the one's as old and ugly as the other! The madwoman hasn't left her room once ever since we've been in this flat.'

'Why does she scream like that?'

'That's just it! It happens when she's left alone in the darkness. She's frightened, like a child. She screams.... I've found out old Mathilde's game at last.... From morning till night she prowls about the passages.... You're always sure to find her behind a door, and when she's caught she hardly turns a hair.... She just moves off, calm as can be, the ugly thing! ... It's got to the point that you don't feel at home in your own place, you have to lower your voice to discuss family matters.... I've just caught her in the act, haven't I? Well! I'm willing to bet she's already come back....'

'That can't be very pleasant,' Maigret agreed. 'But doesn't the landlord do anything about it?'

'He's tried hard to get rid of them.... Unfortunately there are laws.... Besides, it can't be either healthy or pleasant, those two old women in a tiny room.... I'm sure they never wash....'

The Inspector had seized his hat.

'Please forgive me for having disturbed you. It's time I was going....'

Now he had a clear mental picture of their apartment, from the antimacassars on the furniture to the calendars hanging on the walls.

'Don't make a sound!... You'll catch the old woman at it....'

In fact this was not quite the case. She was not in the passage, but behind her half-open door, like a huge spider lying in wait. She must have been taken aback when the Inspector greeted her pleasantly as he went past.

Apéritif time found Maigret sitting in the Select, not far from the American bar where the talk was exclusively about racing. When the waiter came up he showed him the photograph of Roger Couchet which he had taken away from the Hôtel Pigalle that morning.

'D'you know this young man?'

The waiter looked surprised.

'That's odd....'

'What's odd?'

'He left here less than a quarter of an hour ago.... Why, he was at this very table! I shouldn't have noticed him but for the fact that, instead of telling me what he wanted to drink he remarked: "The same as yesterday!" Well, I had no recollection of having seen him ... So I said: "Will you remind me what that was?" "Why, a gin fizz!" And that was what I found so funny! Because I'm sure I never served a single gin fizz yesterday evening.

'He stayed a few minutes, then he went off. . . . It's odd that you should just come and show me his photograph.'

It was not in the least odd. Roger had wanted to make it clear that he had been to the Select the night before, as he had told Maigret. He had used quite a clever trick, and had only made the mistake of choosing a somewhat unusual drink.

A few minutes later Nine came in, looking mournful, and sat down at the table nearest the bar, then, catching sight of the Inspector, she got up, and after a moment's hesitation came over towards him.

'Did you want to speak to me?' she inquired.

'Not specially. Yes, I do, though! I want to ask you a question. You come here most evenings, don't you?'

'This was where Raymond and I always met!'

'Do you always sit in the same place?'

'Over there, where I sat when I came in. . . .'

'Were you there yesterday?'

'Yes, why?'

'And you don't remember seeing the original of this portrait?'

She looked at the photograph of Roger, and murmured:

'But it's the boy from the next room!'

'Yes! It's Couchet's son. . . .'

She stared at him, disturbed by this coincidence and wondering what it might conceal.

'He came to see me soon after you'd left this morning . . . I'd just got back from the Moulin Bleu. . . .'

'What did he want?'

'He asked me if I'd got an aspirin tablet for Céline, who wasn't well. . . .'

'And what about the theatre? Have they signed you on?'

'I'm to go round there tonight. . . . One of the girls has hurt herself. . . . If she's not better I shall take her place, and perhaps they'll take me on permanently. . . .'

She lowered her voice to add:

'I've got the hundred francs. . . . Give me your hand. . . .'

And her gesture was deeply revealing, psychologically. She did not want to offer Maigret the hundred francs in public! She was afraid of embarrassing him! So she held the note, folded very small, in the palm of her hand! She slipped it to him as if to a gigolo!

'Thank you very much! You've been kind. . . .'

She was evidently depressed. She was looking round her without taking the slightest interest in the sight of people coming and going. With the ghost of a smile, however, she remarked:

'The head waiter is looking at us. . . . He's wondering why I'm with you. . . . He must think I've already found a successor to Raymond. . . . You're going to be compromised!'

'Will you have a drink?'

'No thanks!' she said tactfully. 'If you should happen to want me. . . . At the *Moulin Bleu* I'm called Elyane. . . . You know the stage door in the rue Fontaine?'

It was not too much of an ordeal. Maigret rang the doorbell of the flat in the Boulevard Haussmann a little before dinner time. The heavy scent of chrysanthemums greeted him in the entrance hall. The maid who opened the door walked on tiptoe.

She thought the Inspector merely wanted to leave his card, and she led him without a word to the mortuary chamber, all hung with black. By the entrance stood a silver tray full of visiting cards.

The body was already in the coffin, which was piled high with flowers.

In one corner was a tall, elegant young man dressed in mourning, who greeted Maigret with a slight nod.

Opposite him a woman of about fifty was kneeling, coarse-featured, dressed like a peasant in her Sunday best.

The Inspector went up to the young man.

'Might I see Madame Couchet?'

'I'll ask my sister if she can see you.... Your name is?...'

'Maigret! The Inspector in charge of the investigation....'

The country-woman stayed where she was. A few minutes later the young man returned and piloted his guest through the apartment.

Apart from the scent of flowers that prevailed everywhere, there was nothing unusual about the appearance of the rooms. It was a handsome late-nineteenth-century apartment, like most of those along the Boulevard Haussmann. Spacious rooms. Ceilings and doors somewhat over-ornate.

And period furniture. In the drawing-room, a monumental glass chandelier tinkled whenever one walked.

Mme Couchet was there, with three people whom she introduced. First of all the young man in mourning:

'My brother, Henry Dormoy, barrister-at-law....'

Then an elderly gentleman:

'Colonel Dormoy, my uncle....'

Finally a lady with fine silvery hair:

'My mother....'

And they all looked most elegant in their mourning clothes. The tea-table had not yet been cleared, and there were the remains of toast and cakes.

'If you'll kindly sit down....'

'One question, if I may. The lady who is in the mortuary chamber....'

'My husband's sister,' said Madame Couchet. 'She arrived this morning from Saint-Amand....'

Maigret did not smile. But he understood. He was well aware that they were not particularly anxious for members of the Couchet family to turn up looking like peasants or *petits-bourgeois*.

There were the husband's relatives and there were the Dormoy relatives.

The Dormoy relatives were all tact and elegance. Everyone was already wearing black.

So far the Couchet relatives were only represented by that homely matron, whose silk bodice was too tight under the arms.

'Might I have a few words with you in private, madame?'

She apologized to her relatives, who were offering to leave the room.

'Please stay here. ... We can go into the yellow boudoir....'

She had been weeping, quite unmistakably. Then she had powdered her face and one could make out only a slight redness of the eyelids. Her voice was faint with genuine weariness.

'Have you had an unexpected visitor today?'

She raised her head somewhat crossly.

'How did you know? Yes, early this afternoon my stepson came....'

'Did you already know him?'

'Very slightly.... He used to see my husband at his office.... Once, though, at the theatre, we met him and Raymond introduced us to one another....'

'What was the purpose of his visit?'

She turned her head aside in some embarrassment.

'He wanted to know if a will had been found.... He also asked the name of my lawyer, so as to approach him about formalities....'

She sighed, trying to apologize for all these trivialities.

'He's within his rights. I suppose he's entitled to half the fortune, and I've no intention of trying to deprive him....'

'May I ask you a few indiscreet questions?... When you married Couchet, was he already a wealthy man?'

'Yes.... Less so than at present, but he was beginning to get on....'

'A love match?'

A veiled smile.

'You might call it that.... We met at Dinard.... After three weeks, he asked me if I would consent to be his wife. ... My parents made inquiries...'

'Were you happy?'

He was looking her in the eyes, and he had no need of an answer. He chose rather to murmur himself:

'There was quite a difference in your ages.... Couchet had his business.... In short, there was no great intimacy between you.... Wasn't that so?... You kept house for him.... You led your own life and he led his....'

'I never blamed him for it!' she said. 'He was a man of tremendous vitality who needed an eventful life... I never tried to hold him back....'

'You weren't jealous?'

'To begin with.... Then I got used to it.... I think he was very fond of me....'

She was rather pretty, but in a lifeless, colourless way, with somewhat indeterminate features, a soft body, dressed with sober elegance: she must have been a gracious hostess, dispensing tea to her friends in the warm, comfortable drawing-room.

'Did your husband often talk to you about his first wife?'

Then her eyes hardened. She tried to conceal her anger, but she realized that Maigret was not taken in.

'It's hardly my business to...' she began.

'I am sorry. Given the circumstances of his death, there can be no question of delicacy....'

'You don't suspect?...'

'I suspect nobody. I am trying to reconstruct your husband's life, his circle of acquaintance, his actions during that last evening. Did you know that this woman lives in the very building where Couchet had his office?'

'Yes! He told me....'

'How did he speak of her?'

'He had a grudge against her.... Then he would feel ashamed of this feeling and declare that she was really an unhappy creature....'

'Why unhappy?'

'Because nothing could satisfy her.... And also ...'

'And also?...'

'You can guess what I'm trying to say.... She's a very selfish woman.... In short, she left Raymond because he wasn't making enough money.... Then, to meet him again, a rich man ... while she herself was the wife of a petty official!...'

'She didn't try to ...'

'No! I don't think she ever asked him for money. It's true that my husband would never have told me. All I know is that it was agony for him to meet her in the Place des Vosges. I think she used to contrive to run across him. She would never speak at him, but she'd look at him contemptuously....'

The Inspector could not help smiling as he imagined these meetings, under the archway: Couchet getting out of his car, fresh and rosy, and Madame Martin stiff, with her black gloves, her umbrella, and her handbag, her spiteful face....

'That's all you know?'

'He would have liked to change his premises, but it's difficult to find laboratories in Paris....'

'You don't know, of course, if your husband had any enemies?'

'He had none! Everybody loved him! He was too kind, ridiculously kind.... He didn't merely spend money, he threw it away.... And when he was reproached for it he would say that having counted his pennies for years he'd earned the right to be extravagant....'

'Did he see much of your family?'

'Very little!... They hadn't the same mentality, you see ... nor the same tastes....'

Indeed, Maigret found it hard to imagine Couchet in the drawing-room with the young lawyer, the colonel, and the dignified mama.

It was all easy to understand.

A full-blooded, powerful, vulgar fellow, risen from nothing, who had spent thirty years of his life trying to make his fortune, and having a rough time....

He'd grown rich. At last at Dinard he'd gained access to a world into which he had never been admitted. A real *jeune fille*, a young lady ... a bourgeois family....

Tea and *petits fours*, tennis parties and picnics....

He got married! To prove to himself that from now on nothing was beyond his reach! To have a home like those he had seen only from outside!

He got married because he was, furthermore, impressed by this virtuous and well-brought-up young lady....

And then came the flat in the Boulevard Haussmann, with all the traditional trimmings....

Only he felt the need to bestir himself elsewhere, to see different people, to talk to them without self-consciousness ... in brasseries, in bars....

And other women, too!

He was very fond of his wife! He admired her, he respected her, he was in awe of her!

67

But just because he was in awe of her he needed a common girl like Nine to relax with.

Madame Couchet had a question on the tip of her tongue. She seemed reluctant to ask it. Nevertheless she forced herself to, looking away as she spoke.

'I'd like to ask you if.... It's rather delicate.... Excuse me.... He had women friends, I know.... He scarcely made any secret of it, and that only out of delicacy.... I must know if there's likely to be any trouble in that direction, any scandal....'

She obviously imagined her husband's mistresses as novelettish tarts or film vamps.

'You've nothing to be afraid of!' smiled Maigret, remembering little Nine, with her piquant features and the handful of jewels she had taken that very afternoon to the municipal pawn-office.

'It won't be necessary to ...?'

'No! No compensation!'

She was quite amazed at this. Perhaps a trifle hurt, for surely if these women demanded nothing, they must have had a certain fondness for her husband, and he for them....

'Have you fixed the date of the funeral?'

'My brother has seen to that.... It's to be on Thursday, at St Philippe-du-Roule....'

There was a clatter of plates in the dining-room next door. Presumably the table was being laid for dinner.

'It only remains now for me to thank you and take my leave, with renewed apologies ...'

And as he walked down the Boulevard Haussmann he caught himself muttering, while he filled his pipe:

'You old rascal, Couchet!'

The words had sprung to his lips as if Couchet had been an old friend. And he felt this impression so strongly that he could not realize he had only seen him dead.

He felt he knew Couchet from every possible angle.

Perhaps because of the three women?

The first wife, to begin with, the confectioner's daughter in the Nanterre lodgings, in despair at the thought that her husband would never have a respectable job.

Then the young lady from Dinard, and the flattering experience for a man like Couchet of becoming nephew to a Colonel. . . .

Nine. . . . The meetings at the Select. . . . The Hôtel Pigalle. . . .

And the son coming to sponge on him! And Madame Martin contriving to run across him in the entrance-way, hoping perhaps to torture him with remorse. . . .

A queer end to things! All alone, in that office to which he came as seldom as he could! Leaning against the half-open safe, with his hands on the table. . . .

Nobody had noticed anything. . . . As she passed through the courtyard, the concierge had seen him still in the same place behind the frosted window. . . . But she had been chiefly concerned about Madame de Saint-Marc, who was having her baby!

The madwoman had called out, upstairs! In other words, old Mathilde, in her felt slippers, was hiding behind one of the doors in the passage. . . .

Monsieur Martin, in his buff-coloured overcoat, had gone down to hunt for his glove among the dustbins.

One thing was certain: somebody, now, was in possession of the three hundred and sixty thousand stolen francs!

And somebody had committed a murder!

'All men are selfish!' sad-faced Madame Martin had commented bitterly.

Was it she who had the three hundred and sixty brand-new notes handed out by the Crédit Lyonnais? She who at last had money in her possession, plenty of money, a whole bundle of big notes representing years of comfort, free from worry about the morrow or about what pension she would get at Martin's death?

Was it Roger, with his limp body, sapped by ether, and that Céline he had picked up to get stupefied together in a stuffy hotel bedroom?

Was it Nine, or Madame Couchet?...

In any case, there was one spot from which it was possible to have seen everything: the Martins' flat.

And there was a certain woman who prowled about the house, gluing her ear to every door, creeping in slippered feet along the passages.

'I shall have to pay a call on old Mathilde!' Maigret said to himself.

But, next morning, when he reached the Place des Vosges, the concierge, who was sorting the mail (a great pile for the Serum laboratory and a mere handful of letters for the other tenants), stopped him.

'Are you going up to the Martins?... I don't know if you'd better.... Madame Martin was taken horribly ill last night.... They had to send for the doctor.... Her husband's nearly out of his mind....'

The employees were crossing the courtyard, going to start their work in the laboratories and offices. The man-servant was shaking carpets out of a first-floor window.

There was the sound of a baby wailing and a monotonous lullaby chanted by a nurse.

Chapter 6

A Raging Temperature

'Hush!.... She's fallen asleep.... Come in all the same....'

Monsieur Martin shrank back, looking resigned. Resigned to letting the untidiness of his home be seen. Resigned to showing himself in a state of undress, with his moustache drooping and greenish, which indicated that it was usually dyed.

He had stayed up all night. He was exhausted, incapable of any further response.

He went on tiptoe to close the bedroom door, which had disclosed the end of the bed and a basin standing on the floor.

'Did the concierge tell you?'

He was whispering, casting anxious glances at the door. At the same time he turned off the gas, on which he had been heating up some coffee.

'A small cup?'

'No, thank you.... I'm not going to bother you for long.... I wanted to ask after Madame Martin....'

'It's too kind of you!' Martin said with conviction.

He was really quite unsuspecting. He was so upset that he must have lost his critical sense. And indeed, had he ever had it?

'They're terrible, these attacks of hers! ... You don't mind if I drink my coffee? ...'

He became confused on discovering that his braces were dangling about his legs, hastily put his clothes to rights, and cleared the table of several medicine bottles.

'Does Madame Martin have them often?'

'No. . . . Specially not such violent ones! . . . She's very highly strung. . . . When she was a girl, I gather she used to have fits of hysteria every week. . . .'

'Does she still now?'

Martin gave him a hangdog look, and scarcely dared confess:

'I have to be very tactful with her. . . . The slightest contradiction sets her all in a flutter! . . .'

With his buff-coloured overcoat, his well-waxed moustache, his leather gloves, he had chiefly looked ridiculous. The caricature of a pretentious little jack-in-office.

But now his whiskers were faded and there were bags under his eyes. He had not had time to wash. He was still wearing his nightshirt under an old jacket. And he was a pathetic figure. One realized with amazement that he was at least fifty-five years old.

'Did anything upset her, last night?'

'No . . . no. . . .'

He was panic-stricken, darting terrified glances all around him.

'She had no visitors? . . . Her son, for instance? . . .'

'No. . . . You came. . . . Then we had dinner. . . . Then . . .'

'What?'

'Nothing . . . I don't know. . . . It came on without warning. . . . She's very sensitive. . . . She's had so much unhappiness in her life!'

Did he really believe what he was saying? Maigret had the impression that Martin was talking in order to convince himself.

'In short, you've no personal opinion about this crime?'

And Martin dropped the cup he was holding. Could he, too, be suffering from over-sensitive nerves?

'Why should I have an opinion? I give you my word. . . .
If I had one, I'd . . .'

'You would? . . .'

'I don't know. . . . It's terrible! . . . And just when
we've most work on at the office. . . . I haven't even had
time to let my boss know this morning. . . .'

He passed his lean hand across his forehead, then set
about picking up the pieces of china. He spent a long time
hunting for a cloth to wipe the floor.

'If she'd listened to me, we'd never have stayed on in this
house. . . .'

He was frightened, that was obvious. He was convulsed
with fear. But fear of what, fear of whom?

'You're a good fellow, aren't you, Monsieur Martin?
And an honest fellow. . . .'

'I've been in the service thirty-two years and . . .'

'So, if you knew something that might help the law to
discover the criminal, you'd make it your duty to tell
me. . . .'

Weren't his teeth beginning to chatter?

'I'd certainly tell you. . . . But I don't know anything.
. . . And I should like to know, myself! . . . This is no
sort of life . . .'

'What do you think of your stepson?'

Martin looked at Maigret in astonishment.

'Roger? . . . He's . . .'

'He's misguided, I think!'

'But he's not a bad boy, I give you my word. . . . It's
all his father's fault. . . . As my wife always says, young
men ought not to be given so much money. . . . She's
quite right! And I agree with her that Couchet didn't do it
out of kindness nor out of love for his son, who meant
nothing to him. . . . He did it to clear his own conscience. . . .'

'His conscience? . . .'

Martin blushed, more embarrassed than ever.

'He'd behaved badly towards Juliette, hadn't he?' he said in a low voice.

'Juliette?'

'My wife.... His first wife.... What did he ever do for her? Not a thing!... He treated her like a servant.... And yet it was she who helped him through difficult times.... And later on ...'

'He gave her nothing, that's quite true!... But she'd married again. ...'

Martin's face was crimson. Maigret was looking at him with amazement and pity. For he realized that the poor fellow was in no way responsible for this extra-ordinary theory. He was merely repeating what he must have heard his wife say a hundred times.

Couchet was rich, she was poor!... And so ...

But the little official had pricked up his ears.

'Didn't you hear something?'

They kept quiet for a moment. A faint call could be heard from the next room. Martin went to open the door.

'What are you telling him?' Madame Martin demanded.

'Well ... I ...'

'It's the Inspector, isn't it? ... What does he want this time? ...'

Maigret could not see her. The voice was that of some-body lying down, very weary, but none the less completely self-possessed.

'The Inspector called to ask after you. ...'

'Tell him to come in ... Wait a minute! Give me a damp face-cloth and the mirror. And my comb. ...'

'You're going to upset yourself again. ...'

'Hold the mirror straight, can't you!... No! Leave go of it. ... You're incapable of ... Take away that basin! ... Oh, men. ... When a woman's not around, the place looks like a pigsty. ... Bring him in now.'

The bedroom was like the dining-room, drab and dreary, badly furnished, with a lot of old curtains, old covers, faded carpets. As soon as he set foot in the doorway, Maigret felt Madame Martin's gaze fixed on him, calm and extraordinarily lucid.

He saw a sickly invalid's smile appear on her haggard face.

'Don't take any notice,' she said. 'Everything's in a frightful mess! It's because of this attack....'

And she stared sadly in front of her.

'But I'm getting better.... I've got to be well tomorrow, for the funeral.... It is tomorrow, isn't it?...'

'Yes, it's tomorrow! Do you often get these attacks?...'

'I had them when I was a child.... But my sister ...'

'You have a sister?'

'I had two.... Don't go imagining things.... The younger had attacks too.... She got married.... Her husband was a bad lot and one fine day he took advantage of one of these attacks to have her shut up.... She died a week later....'

'Don't get upset!' begged Martin. He didn't know which way to turn or where to look.

'She'd gone out of her mind?' asked Maigret.

And the woman's features hardened again, her voice grew spiteful.

'That's to say her husband wanted to get rid of her!... Less than six months later, he married someone else.... And men are all the same.... You sacrifice yourself, you work yourself to death for them....'

'Please!...' her husband sighed.

'I'm not talking about you! Although you're no better than all the rest....'

And Maigret, suddenly, sensed currents of hatred in the air. The moment was brief. It was nothing definite. And yet he was sure that he was not mistaken.

'All the same, if I'd not been there. . . .' she went on.

Wasn't there a threatening note in her voice? The man was fluttering aimlessly. To hide his confusion, he measured out drops of medicine, letting them fall one by one into a glass.

'The doctor said . . .'

'I don't care what the doctor said!'

'But you must. . . . Here! . . . Drink it slowly. . . . It's not bad. . . .'

She looked at him, then she looked at Maigret, and at last she drank, with a resigned shrug of the shoulders.

'Did you really come just to inquire after me?' she asked suspiciously.

'I was on my way to the laboratory when the concierge told me . . .'

'Have you found out anything?'

'Not yet. . . .'

She closed her eyes to indicate her weariness. Martin looked at Maigret, who got up.

'Well! I hope you'll soon be recovered. . . . You're getting better already. . . .'

She let him go. Maigret stopped Martin from showing him out.

'Stay with her, please.'

Poor fellow! He seemed to be afraid of staying, to be hanging on to the Inspector because, when a third person was there, it was not so bad.

'You'll see, she'll soon be all right. . . .'

As he was crossing the dining-room he heard a gliding step in the passage. And he caught up with old Mathilde, just as she was about to go into her own room.

'Good morning, madame. . . .'

She gave him a frightened look, making no reply, her hand on the door handle.

Maigret had lowered his voice. He guessed that Madame

Martin was listening eagerly, quite capable of getting up to eavesdrop herself.

'As you probably know, I'm the Inspector in charge of the investigation. . . .'

He had already guessed that he would get nothing out of this woman, whose face was so placid that it looked like a full moon.

'What do you want?'

'Merely to ask you if you've anything to tell me. . . . How long have you lived in this house?'

'Forty years!' she replied curtly.

'You know everybody. . . .'

'I don't talk to anybody!'

'I thought you might perhaps have seen or heard something. . . . Sometimes a tiny hint is enough to put the law on the right track. . . .'

Someone was moving about inside the room. But the old woman kept the door stubbornly shut.

'You've not seen anything? . . .'

She made no reply.

'And you've not heard anything? . . .'

'You'd do better to ask the landlord to fix me up with gas. . . .'

'Gas?'

'They've got it in the rest of the house. . . . But because he's not entitled to raise my rent he won't let me have it. . . . He'd like to throw me out! . . . He does all he can to get rid of me. . . . But he'll go out before me, and he'll go out feet first! . . . You can tell him that from me. . . .'

The door opened so slightly that it seemed impossible that the fat old woman could slip through the crack. Then it closed again, and there were only muffled sounds inside the room.

'Have you your card?'

The manservant in his striped waistcoat took the visiting card that Maigret proffered and disappeared into the flat, which was amazingly light, thanks to the fifteen-feet-tall windows that are only to be seen nowadays in houses in the Place des Vosges and the Île Saint-Louis.

The rooms were immense. Somewhere a vacuum cleaner was purring. A nurse in a white overall, with a pretty blue veil on her head, kept going from one room to another and casting curious glances at the visitor.

A voice, close by.

'Ask the Inspector to come in. . . .'

Monsieur de Saint-Marc was in his study, wearing a dressing-gown, his silvery hair neatly smoothed. First he went to close a door through which Maigret had time to glimpse a fine old bed, with a young woman's head on the pillow.

'Sit down, please. . . . Of course, you want to speak to me about that dreadful Couchet affair? . . .'

Despite his age he gave an impression of health and vigour. And the atmosphere of the flat was that of a happy home, where everything is bright and cheerful.

'The tragedy affected me the more especially, as it coincided with a great emotional experience. . . .'

'I've heard about it. . . .'

There was a slight flicker of pride in the eyes of the former ambassador. He was proud of having a child at his age.

'I'll ask you to speak softly, for I'd rather keep the story from Madame de Saint-Marc. . . . In her condition, it would be a pity. . . . But in fact, what do you want to ask me? I scarcely knew the man Couchet. . . . I caught sight of him once or twice as I went through the courtyard. . . . He belonged to one of the clubs I go to occasionally, the Haussmann. But I don't think he often set foot in it. . . . I merely noticed his name in the latest members' list. . . . I believe he was rather a common person, wasn't he? . . .'

'Well, his origins were pretty humble. . . . He'd had quite a struggle to get where he did. . . .'

'My wife told me that he'd married a young woman of very good family, an old schoolfellow of hers. . . . That's one of the reasons why she'd better not be told about it. . . . Well then, you wanted? . . .'

The great windows overlooked the Place des Vosges, brightened by a light burst of sunshine. In the square, gardeners were watering the lawns and flowerbeds. Vans were passing by, drawn by heavy-footed horses.

'A simple piece of information. . . . I know that, in your quite natural state of anxiety at waiting for things, you paced up and down the courtyard many times. . . . Did you meet anyone? . . . Didn't you see anyone going towards the offices at the far end of the courtyard? . . .'

Monsieur de Saint-Marc pondered, while he fingered a paperknife.

'Wait a minute. . . . No! I don't think so. . . . I must admit that I had other things on my mind. . . . The concierge would be better able to . . .'

'The concierge knows nothing. . . .'

'And I myself . . . No! . . . Or rather. . . . But there can't be any connexion . . .'

'Tell me all the same.'

'At a certain moment I heard a noise by the dustbins. . . . I was feeling at a loose end. . . . I went over and saw a woman who lives on the second floor. . . .'

'Madame Martin?'

'I believe that is her name. . . . I must confess that I'm not well acquainted with my neighbours. . . . She was rummaging in one of the galvanized-iron bins. . . . I remember she said to me: "A silver spoon dropped into the rubbish by mistake. . . ." I asked her: "Have you found it?" And she answered, rather quickly: "Yes, yes! . . ."'

'What did she do next?' asked Maigret.

'She hurried back to her own flat. . . . She's a restless little person who's always bustling about. . . . If I remember about it, it's because we once lost a valuable ring that way. . . . And the point is that it was brought back to the concierge by a ragman who found it while poking about with his hook. . . .'

'Can you give me any idea when this incident took place?'

'That's difficult. . . . Wait a minute . . . I didn't feel like eating dinner. . . . But about half past eight Albert, my manservant, begged me to take something. . . . And as I refused to sit down to table, he brought me some anchovy patties in the drawing-room. . . . It was before. . . .'

'Before half past eight?'

'Yes. . . . Let's say that the incident, as you call it, occurred shortly after eight o'clock. . . . But I don't think it can be of the slightest interest. What is your opinion of the affair? . . . For my own part I refuse to believe, as rumour apparently has it, that the crime was committed by one of the residents in the house. . . . Remember that anybody can get into the courtyard. . . . Actually I am going to ask the landlord to see that the main door is closed at dusk. . . .'

Maigret had stood up.

'I have no opinion as yet!' he said.

The concierge was bringing the mail and, as the hall door had been left open, she suddenly caught sight of the Inspector closeted with Monsieur de Saint-Marc. Worthy Madame Bourcier! She was deeply upset! Her look betrayed worlds of anxiety.

Was Maigret going to have the impertinence to suspect the Saint-Marcs? Or even to bother them with his questions?

'Thank you, Monsieur. . . . And please excuse me for paying this call. . . .'

'Cigar?'

Monsieur de Saint-Marc was very much the aristocrat, with a slight touch of condescending familiarity which smacked of the politician rather than of the diplomat.

'I'm entirely at your disposal.'

The manservant closed the door. Maigret walked slowly down the stairs and found himself back in the courtyard, where the delivery man from some big store was looking in vain for the concierge.

In the lodge there were just a dog, a cat and the two children, busily smearing themselves with bread and milk.

'Is your mummy here?'

'She's coming back, m'sieu! She's gone up with the letters. . . .'

In the less respectable corner of the courtyard, close to the lodge, were four galvanized iron bins where, when night fell, the tenants came one after the other to deposit their household rubbish.

At six in the morning the concierge opened the street door and the dustmen emptied the bins into their truck.

At night, this corner was always dark. The only lamp in the courtyard was on the other side, at the foot of the stairs.

What had Madame Martin come to look for, just about the time when Couchet was killed?

Had she, too, taken it into her head to hunt for her husband's glove?

'No!' grunted Maigret, struck by a sudden recollection. 'Martin didn't bring down the rubbish till much later.'

What did it all mean, then? They couldn't have lost a spoon! During the daytime, the tenants were not allowed to deposit anything whatsoever in the empty dustbins!

What had they been hunting for, one after the other?

Madame Martin had been rummaging in the dustbin itself!

And Martin had prowled round it, striking matches!

And next morning the glove had reappeared!

'Did you see the baby?' a voice said behind Maigret.

It was the concierge, speaking of the Saint-Marcs' child with more emotion than of her own.

'You said nothing to madame, I hope? She mustn't be told. . . .'

'I know! I know!'

'About the wreath . . . I mean the tenants' wreath . . . I wonder if it ought to be taken to the Couchets' house today or if it's the custom to leave it only at the time of the funeral. . . . The staff have been very good too. . . . They've collected more than three hundred francs. . . .'

And, turning to a delivery man:

'Who's it for?'

'Saint-Marc!'

'Right-hand staircase. First floor opposite. . . . Mind you ring gently!'

Then, to Maigret:

'If you knew what a lot of flowers she gets! They really don't know where to put them all. They've had to carry most of them up to the servants' rooms. . . . Won't you come in? . . . Jojo, will you please leave your sister alone? . . .'

The Inspector was still staring at the dustbins. What the deuce could the Martins have been hunting for?

'Do you put them out on the pavement in the mornings, according to the regulation?'

'No! Since I lost my husband, I can't manage that! Or else I'd have to pay somebody, for they're far too heavy for me. . . . The dustmen are very obliging. . . . I offer

82

them a drink from time to time and they come in to collect the bins in the yard. . . .'

'So that the ragmen don't get a chance to rummage in them!'

'Don't you believe that! They come into the courtyard too. . . . There's three or four of them sometimes, making no end of a mess. . . .'

'Thank you very much.'

And Maigret went off, deep in thought, forgetting or not bothering to pay another visit to the office, as he had intended that morning.

When he reached the Quai des Orfèvres he was told:

'Somebody's been asking for you on the phone. A Colonel . . .'

But he was still pursuing his train of thought. Opening the door of the detectives' office he called out:

'Lucas! Will you set off immediately. . . . You must question all the dustbin-rakers who usually operate in the neighbourhood of the Place des Vosges. . . . If necessary you must go to the Saint-Denis works where the rubbish is burnt. . . .'

'But . . .'

'We've got to find out if they noticed anything unusual in the dustbins of number 61 Place des Vosges the day before yesterday morning. . . .'

He had let himself sink into his armchair and a word suddenly came back to him: *Colonel*. . . .

What colonel? He didn't know any colonels. . . .

Yes, he did, though! There was one involved in the case! Madame Couchet's uncle! What did he want?

'Hello. . . . Elysée 17–62 . . . Inspector Maigret speaking, Police Headquarters. . . . What did you say? . . . Colonel Dormoy wants to speak to me? . . . Yes, I'm waiting. . . . Hello! Is that Colonel Dormoy? . . . What? . . . A will? . . . I can't hear very well. . . . No, on the contrary, speak a

little softer!... Not quite so close to the mouthpiece....
That's better.... Well then?... You've found an extraordinary will?... And not even sealed?... Right! I'll be around in half an hour.... No, I shan't bother to take a taxi....'

And he lit his pipe, pushing back his armchair and crossing one leg over the other.

Chapter 7

The Three Women

'The Colonel's expecting you, in Monsieur Couchet's room. If you'll kindly follow me. . . .'

The room where the body was lying was now shut. In the neighbouring room, which must have been Madame Couchet's, someone was moving about. The maid opened a door and Maigret saw the Colonel standing beside the table, with his hand resting lightly on it, his chin in the air, as calm and dignified as if he were posing for a sculptor.

'Please sit down!'

Maigret, however, was not taken in; he remained standing and merely unfastened his heavy overcoat, put his bowler hat on a chair and filled his pipe.

'Was it you who found this will?' he asked, looking round the room with interest.

'I found it, this very morning. My niece does not know about it yet. I must say that it's so outrageous. . . .'

A funny kind of room, just like Couchet himself! Certainly the furniture was antique, as in the rest of the apartment. There were a few objects of value. But side by side with them were things that revealed the man's simple tastes.

In front of the window, a table had done service as a desk. There were Turkish cigarettes, but also a whole row of those cherry-wood pipes that cost next to nothing, and which Couchet must have cherished as they matured.

A crimson dressing-gown, the most dazzling he could

find! And then, at the foot of the bed, a pair of old slippers with worn-out soles.

There was a drawer in the table.

'You'll notice that it was not locked,' the Colonel said. 'I don't even know if the key exists. This morning my niece needed some money to pay a tradesman and I wanted to save her the bother of writing a cheque. I had a look in this room. This is what I found. . . .'

An envelope, headed: *Grand Hotel*. Writing paper to match, of a bluish shade.

Then some lines which seemed to have been scribbled down casually, like a rough draft:

This is my last will and testament. . . .

Followed this unexpected sentence:

Since I shall probably forget to inquire about the laws of inheritance, I request my solicitor, Maître Dampierre, to see that my fortune is divided as equally as possible between the following:

my wife Germaine, née Dormoy,
my former wife, now Madame Martin, of 61 Place des Vosges,
Nine Moinard, of Hôtel Pigalle, rue Pigalle.

'What do you think of that?'

Maigret was delighted. This will was the finishing touch that endeared Couchet to him.

'Of course,' the Colonel went on, 'this will won't hold water. There are any number of points that make it invalid, and as soon as the funeral is over we shall contest it. But I thought it important and urgent to tell you about it, because. . . .'

Maigret was still smiling, as if he had been witnessing an amusing practical joke. Even that Grand Hotel writing paper! Like many businessmen who have no office in the city centre, Couchet must have kept some of his appointments there. So, while waiting for somebody, no doubt, in the hall or in the smoking-room, he had picked up a writing pad and scribbled these few lines.

He hadn't closed the envelope! He had flung the whole thing into his drawer, postponing to another time the task of drawing up a formal will.

This had happened a fortnight ago.

'You must have been struck by one really shocking feature,' the Colonel was saying. 'Couchet quite forgets to mention his son! That detail alone is enough to invalidate the will and . . .'

'Do you know Roger?'

'Do I? . . . No. . . .'

And Maigret kept on smiling.

'I was just saying that if I asked you to come here it was because . . .'

'Do you know Nine Moinard?'

The poor man started back as if he'd had his foot trodden on.

'I don't need to know her! Her address, rue Pigalle, is quite enough to tell me. . . . But what was I saying? . . . Oh yes! You saw the date of this will? It's quite recent! . . . Couchet died a fortnight after he'd written it. . . . He was killed! . . . Now suppose one of the two women mentioned here knew the terms of the will. . . . I've every reason to think they're not well off. . . .'

'Why two women?'

'What d'you mean?'

'Three women! The will mentions three women! Couchet's three wives, if you like!'

The Colonel concluded that Maigret must be joking.

'I was speaking seriously. . . .' he said. 'Don't forget there is a dead man in this house! And that the future of a number of people is involved! . . .'

Obviously! All the same, the Inspector felt like laughing. He could not have said why.

'Thank you for telling me about it. . . .'

The Colonel was disappointed. He did not understand how so important an official as Maigret could take such an attitude.

'I suppose that. . . .'

'Good-bye, Colonel Dormoy. . . . Please give my regards to Madame Couchet. . . .'

Out in the street, he could not resist muttering:

'That rascal Couchet!'

So coolly, in all seriousness, he had put down his three women in his will! Including the first, now Madame Martin, who was for ever confronting him with her contemptuous stare, like a living reproach! Including good little Nine, who did her best to cheer him up!

And on the other hand, he forgot that he had a son!

For quite a while, Maigret wondered to whom he should break the news first. To Madame Martin, who would leap out of her bed at the thought of such wealth? To Nine? . . .

'Of course, they've not got the cash yet. . . .'

The thing might drag out for ages. There would be a lawsuit! Madame Martin, in any case, would not give up readily!

'All the same, the Colonel behaved decently! He might have burned the will without anyone being the wiser. . . .'

And Maigret stepped out briskly through the neighbourhood about the Place de l'Europe. Pale sunlight warmed the atmosphere; there was a touch of gaiety in the air.

'That rascal Couchet!'

He went into the lift in the Hôtel Pigalle without stopping at the desk, and a few minutes later was knocking at Nine's door. There was a sound of footsteps inside. The door opened just enough to let through a hand, which remained outstretched in the space.

A woman's hand, shrivelled with age. As Maigret did not move, the hand fluttered impatiently, the face of an elderly Englishwoman appeared above it and a long, incomprehensible speech ensued.

At least, Maigret guessed that the Englishwoman was expecting her mail, which accounted for her gesture. The obvious conclusion was that Nine no longer occupied the room, that she had probably left the hotel.

'Too dear for her!' he reflected.

And he paused, hesitating, before the neighbouring door. A manservant made up his mind for him, by asking suspiciously:

'What d'you want?'

'Monsieur Couchet. . . .'

'Doesn't he answer?'

'I haven't knocked yet.'

And Maigret smiled once again. He was in a cheerful mood. That morning, he suddenly felt as if he were taking part in a practical joke! The whole of life was a joke! Couchet's death was a practical joke, and above all that will of his!

' . . . C'me in!'

The bolt moved. The first thing Maigret did was to draw the curtains and open the windows a little.

Céline had not even woken up. Roger was rubbing his eyes and yawning:

'Oh, so it's you. . . .'

Things had improved. The room no longer smelt of ether. Clothes lay on the floor in a heap.

' . . . D'you want?'

He sat on his bed, took the glass of water from the bedside table and emptied it at one gulp.

'They've found the will!' announced Maigret, drawing the covers over Céline's bare thigh as she lay curled up.

'Well, so what?'

Roger displayed no excitement; barely a touch of curiosity.

'Well, it's a funny sort of will! It'll certainly cause a lot of ink to be spilt and bring the lawyers a lot of money. Just fancy, your father has left his whole fortune to his three women!'

The young man made an effort to understand.

'His three....?'

'Yes! His present legal wife. And then your mother! And finally his girl-friend Nine, who only yesterday was living next door to you! He's asked the lawyer to see that they each get an equal share....'

Roger was unmoved. He seemed to be thinking. But not to be thinking about anything that concerned him personally.

'That's killing!' he said at last in a grave tone that contrasted with his words.

'Just what I said to the Colonel.'

'What Colonel?'

'An uncle of Madame Couchet's.... He's acting the man of the family on her behalf....'

'He must be pulling a face!'

'You're right there!'

The young man thrust his legs out of bed and seized a pair of trousers lying over the back of a chair.

'You don't seem much upset by this news.'

'Oh, as far as I'm concerned....'

He was fastening his trousers, looking for a comb, shutting the window to keep out the chilly air.

'Aren't you in need of money?'

Maigret had suddenly turned serious. His gaze had become weighty, inquisitorial.

'I don't know.'

'You don't know if you're in need of money?'

Roger fixed a glazed stare on the Inspector, who felt suddenly ill at ease.

'I don't give a damn!'

'You've surely not been earning overmuch!'

'I don't earn a penny.'

He yawned, and looked at himself in the glass gloomily. Maigret noticed that Céline had woken up. She wasn't budging. She must have heard part of the conversation, for she was watching the two men with curiosity.

And yet she, too, needed that glass of water! And the atmosphere of the room, with its untidiness, its stale smell, these two demoralized creatures, seemed the quintessence of a defeated world.

'Had you any money saved?'

Roger was beginning to have had enough of this conversation. He looked for his jacket, took out a slender wallet stamped with his initials, and threw it at Maigret.

'Search that!'

Two hundred-franc notes, a few cuttings, a driving licence, and an old cloakroom ticket.

'What will you do if you're done out of your inheritance?'

'I don't want the inheritance!'

'You won't contest the will?'

'No!'

The words had a strange ring. Maigret, who was staring at the carpet, raised his head.

'Three hundred and sixty thousand francs are enough for you?'

Then the young man's attitude changed. He walked up to the Inspector, halting less than a pace away from him so that their shoulders were touching. And he muttered, clenching his fists:

'Say that again!'

At this point there was something of the street bully in his attitude; it suggested brawls in bistros.

'I'm asking you if Couchet's three hundred and sixty thousand francs are. . . .'

He had barely time to grab the other man's arm as it flew out. Otherwise he'd have caught as savage a blow as he'd ever had in his life!

'Calm down!'

Roger, in fact, was calm! He did not struggle. He was pale, with a fixed stare. He was waiting for the Inspector to release him.

Was he going to hit out again? As for Céline, she had leapt out of bed, in spite of being half naked. She was clearly prepared to open the door and call for help.

It all passed off quietly. Maigret only gripped the young man's wrist for a few seconds and, when he allowed him to move freely again, Roger did not stir.

There was a long silence. It seemed as if each hesitated to break it, just as, in a fight, neither man wants to strike the first blow.

In the end it was Roger who spoke.

'You're making the biggest mistake of your life!'

He picked a mauve dressing-gown off the floor and flung it at his companion.

'Will you tell me what you're going to do once you've spent your two hundred francs?'

'What have I done up till now?'

'There's just one little difference: your father is dead and you can't sponge on him any more. . . .'

Roger shrugged his shoulders as if to imply that Maigret understood nothing at all about it.

There was something in the atmosphere that couldn't be pinned down. Not exactly drama. Something different, something distressing! Perhaps it was this unromantic bohemianism? Perhaps that wallet with its two hundred-franc notes?

Or was it the presence of that anxious woman who had

just learnt that tomorrow was going to be different from yesterday and the days before, that she would have to look for a new friend?

No, it wasn't that! It was Roger himself who was frightening! Because his behaviour did not correspond to his past, it contrasted with what Maigret knew about his character!

That calm manner ... And it was not a pose! ... He really was calm, as calm as somebody who. ...

'Give me your revolver!' the Inspector said suddenly.

The young man extracted it from his trouser pocket and held it out with the ghost of a smile.

'You promise me to ....'

He did not finish, for he saw the woman about to scream out in terror. She could not understand. But she felt that something terrible was happening.

There was irony in Roger's eyes.

Maigret practically ran away. He could find nothing more to say, no gesture to make, and he beat a retreat, knocking against the frame of the door as he went out and stifling an oath.

Back in the street, he had lost his earlier good humour. Life had ceased to seem like a joke. He raised his head to look up at the couple's window. It was shut. There was nothing to be seen.

He felt uneasy, as one suddenly feels when one has ceased to understand.

Once or twice, there had been a look in Roger's eyes. ... He could not have explained it. ... But it was not the sort of look he had expected. ... It was a look that did not fit in with the rest of the picture. ...

He retraced his steps, because he had forgotten to ask at the hotel for Nine's new address.

'Don't know!' said the porter. 'She paid for her room and she went off with her suitcase! She didn't need a taxi. . . . She must have picked a cheaper hotel in the neighbourhood. . . .'

'Look here . . . if . . . if anything should happen in your place. . . . Yes . . . anything unexpected . . . I'd like you to get in touch with me personally at Police Headquarters . . . Inspector Maigret. . . .'

He was vexed with himself for having done that. What was likely to happen? All the same, he kept thinking of the two hundred-franc notes in the wallet and the frightened look in Céline's eyes.

A quarter of an hour later he went into the Moulin Bleu through the stage door. The house was empty, dark, the stalls and the edges of the boxes covered with shiny green material.

On the stage six women, shivering in spite of their coats, were rehearsing the same ridiculously simple steps over and over again, while a fat little man shouted himself hoarse, yelling out a tune.

'One! . . . Two! . . . Tra la la la . . . No, no! . . . Tra la la la. . . . Three! . . . Three, for God's sake!'

Nine was the second of these women. She had recognized Maigret, who was standing beside a pillar. The man had seen him too, but didn't care.

'One! . . . Two! . . . Tra la la la. . . .'

This went on for a quarter of an hour. It was colder than outside, and Maigret's feet were frozen. At last the little man mopped his brow and yelled an insult to his troupe by way of farewell.

'Did you want me?' he shouted to Maigret.

'No! . . . I wanted . . .'

Nine came towards him, ill at ease, wondering if she should offer her hand to the Inspector.

'I've some important news to tell you. . . .'

'Not here. . . . We're not allowed to have visitors in the

theatre.... Except at night, because it brings customers....'

They sat down at a small table in a near-by bar.

'Couchet's will has been found.... He leaves all his
fortune to three women....' She was looking at him in
astonishment, without suspecting the truth.

'His first wife for one, although she's remarried....
Then his second wife.... Then you....'

She kept her eyes fixed on Maigret, who saw them widen
and then mist over.

And at last she hid her face in her hands and wept.

Chapter 8

The Sick-Nurse

'He had heart trouble. He knew it.'

Nine took a sip of her ruby-red apéritif.

'That's why he took care of himself. He said he'd done enough work, it was time for him to enjoy life. . . .'

'Did he sometimes talk about death?'

'Often! . . . But not about . . . that sort of death! He was thinking of his heart trouble. . . .'

They were in one of those small bars patronized only by regular customers. The bartender was looking slyly at Maigret, whom he took for a bourgeois on a spree. At the counter they were discussing that afternoon's racing.

'Was he depressed?'

'It's hard to explain! Because he wasn't an ordinary sort of man. For instance, we'd be at the theatre, or somewhere like that. He'd be enjoying himself. Then, for no reason, he'd say with a big sigh: "It's a lousy life, eh, Ninette?"'

'Was he interested in his son?'

'No. . . .'

'Did he talk about him?'

'Hardly ever! Only when he'd been to sponge on him.'

'And what did he say then?'

'He'd give a sigh: "What a hopeless fool! . . ."'

Maigret had already sensed it: for one reason or another, Couchet had had little fondness for his son. He even seemed to have been sickened by the young man. Sickened to the point of not trying to pull him through!

For he had never lectured him. And he gave him money to get rid of him, or out of pity.

'Waiter! What do I owe you?'

'Four francs sixty!'

Nine went out with him and they paused for a moment on the pavement of the rue Fontaine.

'Where are you living now?'

'Rue Lepic, the first hotel on the left. I haven't seen what its name is yet. It's fairly clean. . . .'

'When you're rich, you'll be able to. . . .'

She gave a tearful smile.

'You know I shan't ever be rich! I'm not that type. . . .'

The strange thing was that Maigret had exactly the same feeling! Nine didn't look the type who would ever be rich! He could not have said why.

'I'll go along with you as far as the Place Pigalle, where I catch my bus.'

They walked slowly, the huge, heavy man, and the girl looking fragile by the side of her companion's broad back.

'If you knew how lost I feel all by myself! Luckily there's the theatre, with rehearsals twice a day till the new revue's ready. . . .'

She had to take two steps to Maigret's one, so that she was almost running. At the corner of the rue Pigalle she suddenly stopped, while the Inspector frowned and muttered between his teeth:

'The fool!'

And yet they could not see what had happened. Opposite the Hotel Pigalle was a crowd of some forty people. A policeman, in the doorway, was trying to move people on.

That was all! But there was that special atmosphere, that silence that only reigns in a street when something disastrous has taken place.

97

'What's happened?' stammered Nine. 'At my hotel! . . .'

'No! It's nothing! You go home. . . .'

'But . . . if. . . .'

'Go home!' he ordered sharply.

And she obeyed, frightened, while the Inspector forced his way through the crowd. He bore down on it like a battering ram. Women abused him. The policeman recognized him and took him into the hallway of the hotel.

The District Inspector was already there, talking to the porter, who looked at Maigret and cried:

'That's him! . . . I recognize him! . . .'

The two policemen shook hands. Sobs and moans and a confused murmur of voices could be heard from a small sitting-room that opened into the hall.

'How did he do it?' asked Maigret.

'The woman who lives with him says that he was standing in front of the window, quite calm. She was getting dressed. He was watching her and whistling. He just broke off whistling to tell her that she had nice thighs, but that her calves were too thin. . . . Then he began whistling again. . . . And suddenly she heard nothing more. . . . She had an agonizing sensation of emptiness. . . . He wasn't there any more! . . . He couldn't have gone out through the door . . .'

'Right! Did he hurt anyone when he fell on the pavement?'

'Nobody! Killed outright! His spine broken in two places. . . .'

'They've come!' announced the policeman.

And the District Inspector explained to Maigret:

'The ambulance. . . . There's nothing else to be done. . . . D'you know if there are any relatives to be told? . . . When you turned up the porter was just telling me the young man had had a visitor this morning. . . . A big, tall man. . . . He was just describing the man when I saw you.... It was you! ... Am I to make a report all the same, or are you going to take charge of everything?'

'Make a report.'

'And what about the family?'

'I'll see to that.'

He pushed open the sitting-room door, and saw a figure stretched on the floor, entirely shrouded in a coverlet taken from one of the beds.

Céline, slumped in an armchair, was now keeping up a steady wailing, while a stout woman, the proprietor's wife or the manageress, was lavishing consolation on her.

'It's not as if he'd killed himself on your account, is it? ... You couldn't have stopped it.... You never refused him anything....'

Maigret did not lift the coverlet, did not even show himself to Céline.

A few moments later, the body was being carried to the ambulance, which then drove off towards the Institute of Forensic Medicine.

Then, little by little, the crowd in the rue Pigalle broke up. Inquisitive latecomers did not even know whether there had been a fire, a suicide or the arrest of a pickpocket.

'He was whistling.... And suddenly she heard nothing more....'

Maigret went slowly, very slowly up the staircase in the Place des Vosges, and the nearer he drew to the second floor the glummer he became.

Old Mathilde's door was ajar. No doubt the woman was standing behind it, keeping watch. But he shrugged his shoulders and pulled the cord that hung in front of the Martins' door.

His pipe was in his mouth. For a moment he considered

putting it in his pocket, then, once again, shrugged his shoulders.

There was a clink of bottles. A confused murmur. Two men's voices drawing nearer, and at last the door opening.

'All right, doctor.... Yes, doctor.... Thank you, doctor....'

A dejected Monsieur Martin, who had not yet had time to tidy himself up and faced Maigret in the same bedraggled state as that morning.

'It's you?...'

The doctor made his way towards the staircase, while Monsieur Martin showed the Inspector in, casting a furtive glance into the bedroom.

'Is she worse?'

'We don't know.... The doctor doesn't want to commit himself.... He's coming back tonight....'

He picked up a prescription from the radio, and stared at it blankly.

'I haven't even got anyone to send to the chemist's!'

'What happened?'

'Much the same as last night, only worse.... She began to shake, and to mutter incomprehensible things.... I sent for the doctor and he says she's got a very high temperature....'

'Is she delirious?'

'I tell you, one can't understand what she's saying! We ought to have some ice, and a rubber thing for putting it on her forehead....'

'Would you like me to stay here while you go to the chemist's?'

Monsieur Martin was on the point of refusing. Then he gave in.

He put on an overcoat and went out gesticulating, a grotesque and tragic figure, then came back because he had forgotten to take any money.

Maigret had no ulterior motive in staying in the flat. He showed no interest in anything, did not open a single drawer, did not even glance at a pile of letters lying on a table.

He heard the irregular breathing of the sick woman who, from time to time, heaved a deep sigh, then babbled some mixed-up syllables.

When Monsieur Martin returned he found Maigret in the same place.

'Have you got all you need?'

'Yes. . . . It's terrible! . . . And I haven't even told them at the office! . . .'

Maigret helped him to break up the ice and put it into the red rubber bag.

'You didn't have any visitors this morning, did you?'

'Nobody. . . .'

'And you got no letters?'

'Nothing. . . . Some circulars. . . .'

Madame Martin's forehead was bathed in sweat and her greying hair clung to her temples. Her lips were dis-coloured. But her eyes remained amazingly alive.

Did they recognize Maigret, who was holding the bag over the patient's head?

One couldn't tell. But she seemed a little calmer. With the red ice-bag on her forehead, she lay still, staring at the ceiling.

The Inspector drew Monsieur Martin back into the dining-room.

'I've got several pieces of news for you.'

'Oh?' he said with a shudder of anxiety.

'Couchet's will has been found. He has left one third of his fortune to your wife.'

'What?'

And Martin became flustered, as though bewildered and disconcerted by the news.

'You say he's left us ...?'

'One third of his fortune! I don't expect it'll be plain sailing. His second wife is bound to contest it. . . . For she only gets a third herself. . . . The remaining third goes to somebody else, Couchet's last mistress, a girl called Nine. . . .'

Why did Martin seem so distressed? Worse than distressed! Appalled! He seemed completely paralysed by the news. He was staring at the floor, unable to get a grip on himself.

'The other piece of news is not so good. . . . It's about your stepson. . . .'

'Roger?'

'He killed himself this morning by jumping out of the window of his room in the rue Pigalle . . .'

Then he saw little Martin bristle up and glare at him furiously, shouting:

'What are you talking about? . . . You want to drive me mad, don't you? . . . Confess that it's all a trick to get me to speak! . . .'

'Not so loud! . . . Your wife . . .'

'I don't care! . . . You're lying! . . . It isn't possible . . .'

He was unrecognizable. He had suddenly lost all his timidity, all the good breeding on which he set so much store.

And it was strange to see his distorted face, his trembling lips, his hands fluttering about in the air.

'I give you my word,' Maigret insisted, 'that both these pieces of news are official. . . .'

'But why should he have done that? . . . It's enough to drive one mad, I tell you! . . . Besides, that's what's actually happening! . . . My wife's going mad! . . . You've seen her! . . . And if this goes on I shall go mad too! . . . We shall all go mad! . . .'

His eyes were feverishly restless. He had lost all self-control.

'Her son's jumped out of the window! ... And the will ...'

All his features were contracted and suddenly there was an outburst of weeping, tragic, comic, horrible.

'Please try and keep calm!'

'My whole life.... Thirty-two years.... Every day.... At nine o'clock.... Never incurred a reproof.... And all that for ...'

'Please.... Remember that your wife can hear you, and that she's very ill....'

'And what about me? ... D'you think I'm not ill too? ... D'you think that I can put up with this sort of life much longer? ...'

He hardly looked the weeping sort, and that was just what made his tears so pathetic.

'It's no fault of yours, is it? ... He was only your stepson.... You're not responsible....'

Martin looked at the Inspector, suddenly quietened, but not for long.

'I'm not responsible ...'

He flared up again.

'All the same I'm the one who has all the worry! You come here and tell these stories! ... On the staircase the other tenants give me dirty looks ... I bet they suspect me of having killed that Couchet.... That's it! ... And besides, how am I to know that you don't suspect me too? ... What are you doing here? ... Aha! You don't answer! ... You wouldn't dare answer.... It's always the weakest who's picked on.... A man who can't defend himself.... And my wife's ill.... And ...'

Waving his arms about, he struck the radio set with his elbow, and it toppled over and crashed to the floor with a loud noise of smashed valves.

Then the petty official reappeared.

'A set that cost me twelve hundred francs! ... I had to wait three years before I could afford it....'

A moan came from the neighbouring room. He listened attentively, but did not move.

It was Maigret who glanced into the room. Madame Martin was still prostrate. The Inspector met her gaze, and he could not have said whether it reflected keen intelligence or feverish unease.

She made no attempt to speak. She let him go away.

In the dining-room, Martin had propped both elbows on a sideboard, and was holding his head in his hands, staring at the tapestry that hung a few inches from his face.

'Why should he have killed himself?'

'Suppose for instance that it was he who....'

Silence. A crackling sound. A strong smell of burning. Martin had noticed nothing.

'Is there something on the stove?' inquired Maigret.

He went into the kitchen, which was blue with smoke. On the gas stove he found a saucepan of milk which had boiled over and seemed in danger of disintegrating. He turned off the gas, opened the window, catching sight of the courtyard, the Serum laboratory, and the director's car parked at the foot of the steps. He could hear the tapping of typewriters in the offices.

If Maigret lingered, there was a reason. He wanted to give Martin time to quieten down, to get hold of himself. He slowly filled his pipe and lit it with a lighter hanging above the stove.

When he returned to the dining-room the man had not moved, but he had grown calmer. He stood up with a sigh, hunted for a handkerchief and blew his noise noisily.

'All this is going to end badly, isn't it?' he began.

'There have been two deaths already!' Maigret replied. 'Two deaths....'

An effort. An effort which must have been agonizing, for Martin, who had been on the verge of a new outburst, managed to control his nerves.

'In that case, I think it would be better . . .'

'It would be better? . . .'

The Inspector hardly dared speak. He held his breath. His heart was beating faster, for he felt he was quite close to the truth.

'Yes. . . .' Martin mumbled to himself. 'Can't be helped! . . . It's essential . . . es . . . sen . . . tial. . . .'

Nevertheless, he walked mechanically as far as the open door of the bedroom and looked in.

Maigret was still waiting, motionless and silent.

Martin said nothing. His wife's voice was not heard. Even so something must have taken place.

The situation seemed as though it would go on for ever. The Inspector began to grow impatient.

'Well? . . .'

The man turned slowly towards him, with a new expression.

'What?'

'You were saying that . . .'

Monsieur Martin attempted to smile.

'That what?'

'That it would be better, in order to avoid further tragedies . . .'

'That what would be better?'

He passed his hand across his forehead like someone who finds it hard to revive his memories.

'I beg your pardon! I'm so upset . . .'

'That you've forgotten what you were going to say?'

'Yes . . . I don't know. . . . Look! . . . She's asleep. . . .'

He pointed to Madame Martin, who had closed her eyes; her face had turned crimson, doubtless as a result of the pack of ice applied to her forehead.

'What do you know?' asked Maigret, in the tone he would use to an over-cunning suspect.

'Me?'

And henceforward all his answers were going to be like that! Acting half-witted. Repeating a word in astonishment.

'You were just about to tell me the truth....'

'The truth?'

'Come now! Don't try and make yourself out an idiot. You know who killed Couchet....'

'Me? ... *I* know? ...'

If he had never had a slap in the face, he narrowly escaped getting a tremendous one then from Maigret!

The latter, his lips tight, was looking at the woman who lay there motionless, asleep or pretending to sleep, and then at the little man with his eyelids still swollen, his features haggard from his recent upset, and his moustache drooping.

'You'll take sole responsibility for whatever happens?'

'What's likely to happen?'

'You're making a mistake, Martin!'

'What sort of mistake?'

What had happened? During the space of one minute, perhaps, the man who had been about to talk had stood between the two rooms, with his eyes fixed on his wife's bed. Maigret had heard nothing. Martin had not moved.

Now she had gone to sleep! He was pretending to be innocent.

'Please excuse me ... I think at times I'm not in my right mind.... You must admit it's enough to drive one crazy....'

All the same he still seemed depressed and even gloomy. He looked like a condemned man. His eyes avoided Maigret's, hovered over familiar objects, finally fastened on the radio set, which he proceeded to pick up, crouching on the floor with his back to the Inspector.

'What time is the doctor coming?'

'I don't know. . . . He said tonight. . . .'

Maigret went out, slamming the door behind him. He found himself face to face with old Mathilde, who was so taken aback that she stood motionless and open-mouthed.

'You've got nothing to tell me either, have you, eh? . . . I suppose you're going to claim that you know nothing either? . . .'

She tried to recover her self-possession. She kept both hands under her apron, automatically assuming the attitude of an old housewife.

'Let's go into your place. . . .'

She dragged her felt slippers across the floor, then paused, reluctant to push her half-open door.

'Come on! In you go. . . .'

And Maigret went in after her, kicked the door to, and never even cast a glance at the crazy woman who was sitting by the window.

'Now then, speak up! . . . Understand? . . .'

And he subsided heavily on to a chair.

Chapter 9

The Man with a Pension

'For one thing, they spend their lives quarrelling!'

Maigret did not bat an eyelid. He was up to the neck in this everyday squalor which was more sickening than the drama itself.

The old woman facing him wore an appallingly jubilant and menacing expression. She was talking! She was going on talking! Out of hatred for the Martins, for the dead man, for all the tenants in the house, out of hatred for the whole of mankind! And out of hatred for Maigret!

She stood there with her hands clasped over her great flabby stomach. She seemed to have been waiting all her life for this moment.

It was not merely a smile that drifted across her lips. It was actual bliss, melting her whole being!

'*For one thing*, they spend their whole lives quarrelling.'

She was in no hurry. She was measuring out her phrases. She was taking her time to express her contempt for people who quarrel.

'Worse than guttersnipes! And it's been going on for ever! So that I wonder he's not put an end to her before now.'

'Oh! so you were expecting? . . .'

'When you live in a house like this one, you can expect anything. . . .'

She was guarding the inflexions of her voice. Was she more odious than absurd, or more absurd than odious?

The room was large. There was an unmade bed, with

grey sheets that must never have hung out to dry in the open air. A table, an old cupboard, a stove.

In an armchair, the madwoman, who was staring straight ahead with a faint fond smile.

'Tell me, do you sometimes have visitors?' asked Maigret.

'Never!'

'And your sister never leaves this room?'

'Sometimes she escapes to the stairs....'

A discouraging greyness. A smell of squalid poverty, of old age, possibly a smell of death?

'Notice that it's always the wife who does the attacking!'

Maigret scarcely felt strong enough to question her. He looked at her vaguely. He was listening.

'About money matters, of course! Never anything to do with women.... Although once when she was doing the accounts and she thought that he'd been to a certain sort of house, she let him have it....'

'Does she beat him?'

Maigret's question was not ironical. The suggestion was no more absurd than any other. The whole situation was so unreal that nothing could seem surprising any longer.

'I don't know if she beats him, but in any case she smashes crockery.... Then she begins to cry, and says he'll never have a decent home....'

'In a word, there are scenes practically every day?'

'Not big scenes! But nagging. Two or three big scenes a week....'

'It keeps you busy?'

She was not sure of having caught his meaning and looked at him with a shade of anxiety.

'What does she usually nag him about?'

'"A man ought not to get married if he can't provide for his wife!"

'"A man ought not to deceive a woman by leading her

to believe he's going to get promotion when it isn't true. . . ."

'"Taking a woman away from a man like Couchet, who's capable of making millions! . . ."

'"You officials are poor-spirited creatures. . . . A man has got to work on his own, to enjoy taking risks, to have some initiative, if he wants to get anywhere. . . ."'

Poor Martin, with his gloves, his buff overcoat, his waxed moustache! Maigret could imagine all the phrases that would come drizzling or pouring down on his head.

He'd done what he could, though! Before him, Couchet had incurred the same reproaches. And Couchet must have been told:

'Just look at Monsieur Martin! There's an intelligent man for you! And he thinks he may get married one of these days! And his wife will have a pension if anything should happen to him! Whereas you . . .'

It all looked like a sinister caricature! Madame Martin had been mistaken, she'd been taken in, she'd taken in everybody else!

There was an appalling mistake at the bottom of it.

The confectioner's daughter from Meaux wanted money. That was an established fact! Money was a necessity. She knew it! She was born to have money and therefore it was her husband's duty to make money!

Suppose Couchet did not make enough? And she wouldn't even get a pension if he died?

Then she would marry Martin! That was that!

Only Couchet was the one who became a millionaire, when it was too late! And there was no hope of spurring on Martin, no way of inducing him to leave the Wills and Probate Office and start selling serums, or something equally profitable!

She was unfortunate! She had always been unfortunate! Life seemed to delight in disappointing her hideously.

Old Mathilde's eyes, grey-green as jellyfish, were fixed on Maigret.

'Did her son come to see her?'

'Sometimes.'

'Did she make scenes with him too?'

You would have thought the old woman had been waiting for this moment for years. She was taking her time. She was in no hurry!

'She used to give him advice . . .

'"Your father's rich! He ought to be ashamed of not fixing you up better! You haven't even got a car. . . . And d'you know why? Because of that woman who married him for his money! For that was all she married him for. . . .

'"Not to mention that heaven knows what she's planning against you. . . . D'you expect you'll get a penny of the fortune that's due to you? . . .

'"That's why you ought to get some money out of him now, and put it aside in a safe place. . . .

'"I'll keep it for you, if you like. . . . Tell me! Wouldn't you like me to keep it for you? . . ."'

And Maigret, staring at the grimy floor, pondered, with a grim frown.

Amidst that jumble of feelings he thought he could recognize one feeling that dominated, that had perhaps given rise to all the rest: anxiety! A morbid, unhealthy anxiety, verging on madness. . . .

Madame Martin was always talking about what might happen: her husband's death, her destitution if he left her without a pension. . . . She worried about her son's future too! . . .

It was a nightmare, an obsession.

'What did Roger reply?'

'Nothing! He never stayed long! He must have had something better to do elsewhere. . . .'

'Did he come on the day of the murder?'

'I don't know.'

And in her corner the madwoman, as old as Mathilde, was still staring at the Inspector with an engaging smile.

'Did the Martins have a more interesting conversation than usual?'

'I don't know.'

'Did Madame Martin come downstairs about eight o'clock that evening?'

'I don't remember! I can't be in the passage the whole time.'

Was it unawareness, or transcendent irony? In any case she was keeping something back. Maigret could feel it. All the poison hadn't come out yet!

'They had a quarrel that evening. . . .'

'What about?'

'I don't know. . . .'

'Didn't you listen?'

She made no reply. Her face seemed to say: That's my own business!

'What else do you know?'

'I know why she's ill!'

And that was the moment of triumph! Her hands, still clasped across her stomach, were quivering. The culminating point of her whole career!

'Why?'

This had to be savoured.

'Because. . . . Wait while I ask my sister if she needs anything. . . . Fanny, aren't you thirsty? . . . Hungry? . . . Too hot? . . .'

The small cast-iron stove was glowing. The old woman glided about the room on her noiseless felt soles.

'Because?'

'Because he didn't bring back the money!'

She uttered this sentence deliberately, and followed it up

with a heavy silence. That was the end! She'd stop talking! She had said enough.

'What money?'

Waste of time! She would answer no more questions.

'It's none of my business! That was what I heard! Make what you like of it. . . . Now it's time for me to look after my sister. . . .'

He went off, leaving the two old women engaged in heaven knows what ministrations.

It had made him feel quite ill. He was utterly nauseated, as though from seasickness.

'*He didn't bring back the money. . . .*'

Couldn't it all be explained? Martin must have made up his mind to rob the former husband, perhaps so as to incur no more reproaches for his mediocrity. She would have watched him through the window. He'd come out with the three hundred and sixty bank notes. . . .

Only when he came back he hadn't got them with him! Had he put them away in a safe place somewhere? Had he been robbed himself? Or had he taken fright and got rid of the money by throwing it into the Seine?

Had he committed a murder? Ordinary little Monsieur Martin in his buff overcoat?

He had been anxious to talk, a short while ago. His weariness was surely that of a guilty man who no longer feels strong enough to keep quiet, who prefers immediate imprisonment to the agony of suspense.

But why was it his wife who was ill?

And, above all, why was it Roger who killed himself?

And wasn't the whole thing a figment of Maigret's imagination? Why not suspect Nine, or Madame Couchet, or even the Colonel?

The Inspector, walking slowly down the stairs, ran into Monsieur de Saint-Marc, who turned round.

'Hello, it's you. . . .'

He held out a condescending hand.

'Anything fresh? D'you think we shall be clear of it all?'

And then a cry from the madwoman upstairs, whose sister must have deserted her to take up her post behind some door or other!

An impressive funeral. A large congregation. Highly respectable people, especially Madame Couchet's relations and the neighbours from the Boulevard Haussmann.

In the front row, only Couchet's sister did not quite fit in, although she had done her utmost to look smart. She was in tears. Above all she had a noisy way of blowing her nose that each time earned her an angry look from the dead man's mother-in-law.

Immediately behind the family, the staff from the Serum laboratory.

And with the staff, old Mathilde, looking very dignified, very sure of herself and of her right to be there.

The black dress she was wearing must have been kept for that sole purpose: to go to funerals! Her eyes met Maigret's. And she deigned to give him a slight nod.

Organ music broke forth, the precentor's bass, the deacon's falsetto: '*Et ne nos inducat in tentationem . . .*'

The sound of chairs being pushed back. The hearse was a high one and yet it was completely hidden under flowers and wreaths.

From the tenants of 61 Place des Vosges.

Mathilde must have contributed. Had the Martins put their names on the subscription list too?

Madame Martin was not to be seen. She was still in bed.

'*Libera nos, Domine . . .*'

The absolution. The end. . . . The chief usher slowly led out the procession. In a corner, near a confessional box, Maigret discovered Nine; her little nose was red, but she had not bothered to powder it.

114

'It's terrible, isn't it?' she said.

'What's terrible?'

'Everything! I don't know! That music … And that smell of chrysanthemums. …'

She bit her lower lip to check a sob.

'You know … I've been thinking a lot. … Well! I sometimes wonder if he hadn't been suspecting something. …'

'Are you going to the cemetery?'

'What d'you think? I might be seen, mightn't I? … Perhaps I'd better not go. … And yet I'd so much like to know where they're putting him. …'

'You've only to ask the caretaker.'

'Yes. …'

They were speaking in whispers. The footsteps of the last members of the congregation died away on the other side of the door. Cars started off.

'You were saying he suspected something?'

'Maybe not that he'd die the way he did. … But he knew he wouldn't last much longer. … He had serious heart trouble. …'

It was obvious that she had been worrying about it, that for hours and hours her mind had been occupied with a single theme.

'Things he said, that keep coming back to me. …'

'Was he afraid?'

'No! Rather the reverse. … When anyone happened to mention a graveyard, he'd say with a laugh: "The only place where you can be quiet. … A cosy little corner in the Père-Lachaise. …"'

'Did he often joke?'

'Specially when he wasn't feeling cheerful. … You understand? … He didn't like people to see that he had worries. … At times like that he'd look for any excuse to be lively and have a laugh. …'

'When he talked about his first wife, for instance?'

'He never talked about her to me.'

'Or about the second?'

'No! He didn't talk about anyone in particular. . . . Just about people in general. . . . He thought they were a funny sort of creature. . . . If a waiter robbed him in a restaurant he'd give him a particularly affectionate look; "A scoundrel!" he'd say.'

'And he'd look quite pleased and happy as he said it!'

It was cold. Regular Hallowe'en weather. Maigret and Nine had nothing to do in the Saint-Philippe-du-Roule district.

'How are things at the Moulin Bleu?'

'All right!'

'I'll come and see you there some evening soon. . . .'

Maigret shook her hand and jumped on to the platform of a bus.

He wanted to be alone, to think, or rather to let his thoughts wander. He imagined the procession, which would soon have reached the cemetery . . . Madame Couchet . . . the Colonel . . . the brother. . . . People talking about that strange will. . . .

'What were they after, round those dustbins? . . .'

For that was the crux of the drama. Martin had prowled round the dustbins under pretext of looking for a glove, which he had not found, and yet he had been wearing next morning. Madame Martin had also ransacked the rubbish, saying that a silver spoon had been thrown away by mistake.

'. . . *Because he didn't bring back the money* . . .' old Mathilde had said.

Actually, things must be cheerful at the Place des Vosges just now! Was the madwoman, left by herself, screaming as usual?

The crowded bus, sped past the stops. Somebody close to Maigret was saying to his neighbour:

'Did you read that story about the thousand-franc notes?'

'No! What was that?'

'Wish I'd been there. . . . At the Bougival lock the morning before yesterday. . . . Thousand-franc notes floating down the stream. . . . A waterman was the first to spot them, and he managed to fish up a few. . . . But the lock-keeper realized what had happened. . . . He sent for the police. . . . So they put a cop to keep his eye on people fishing for loot. . . .'

'Not really? That can't have stopped them from pinching a few on the sly. . . .'

'The paper says they've recovered about thirty notes, but that there must have been many more, because a couple were fished up at Mantes too. . . . What d'you say to that? Notes swimming all down the Seine. . . . Better than gudgeon, eh? . . .'

Maigret did not move a muscle. He was a head taller than anyone else. His face was placid.

'. . . *Because he didn't bring back the money* . . .'

So that was it? Little Monsieur Martin, seized with terror or remorse at the thought of his crime? Martin, who admitted having gone for a walk on the Île Saint-Louis that evening to clear his head! . . .

Maigret gave a faint smile, however, when he pictured Madame Martin witnessing the whole thing from her window and waiting.

Her husband must have come back weary and depressed. She'd have watched his every action. She'd expect to see the notes, perhaps to count them. . . .

He'd have undressed, got ready for bed.

Didn't she go and pick up his clothes then and hunt through the pockets?

Anxiety would dawn. She would stare at Martin with his mournful moustache.

'*The . . . the . . . the money!*'

'*What money?*'

'*Who did you give it to? Answer me! . . . Don't try to lie!*'

And Maigret, as he got off the bus at the Pont-Neuf, from which he could see the windows of his office, caught himself saying half aloud:

'I bet Martin burst into tears in his bed! . . .'

Chapter 10

Cards of Identity

Things started to happen at Jeumont. It was eleven o'clock at night. A few third-class travellers were making their way towards the customs office, while the officials began their tour of inspection of the second and first-class carriages.

Meticulous people were preparing their luggage in advance, spreading things out on the seat. One was a man with worried eyes, in a second-class compartment where he was alone except for an elderly Belgian couple.

His luggage was a model of order and forethought. The shirts had been wrapped in paper to keep them clean. There were a dozen pairs of cuffs, warm pants and summer pants, an alarm clock, shoes and a pair of tired-looking slippers.

A woman's hand was obvious in the arrangement. Not a corner had been wasted. Nothing could get crumpled. A customs official turned the things over with a careless hand, his eye on the man in the buff overcoat who looked just the type to own that sort of luggage.

'O.K.'

A cross scribbled in chalk on the cases.

'You people got anything to declare?'

'Excuse me!' the man asked. 'Where exactly does Belgium begin?'

'You see the first hedge over there? No, you can't see anything! But look.... Count the lights.... The third on the left.... Well, that's the frontier....'

A voice in the corridor, repeating at every door:

'Passports and identity cards ready, please!'

And the man in the buff overcoat was struggling to put his cases back on the rack.

'Passport?'

He turned round, saw a young man wearing a grey hat.

'French? ... Your identity card, then. ...'

That took a few moments. His fingers fumbled in his wallet.

'Here, monsieur!'

'Right! Edgar Émile Martin. ... That's it. ... Follow me. ...'

'Where? ...'

'You can bring your cases. ...'

'But ... the train ...'

The Belgian couple were staring at him now in alarm, thrilled none the less at having travelled with a malefactor. Monsieur Martin, his eyes starting out of his head, climbed on to the seat to take down his cases again.

'I swear to you ... Whatever ...?'

'Hurry up. ... The train's about to leave. ...'

And the young man in the grey hat trundled the heaviest of the cases on to the platform. It was pitch black. Under the lamplight people were hurrying back from the refreshment room. The whistle blew. A woman was arguing with the customs officials, who prevented her from leaving.

'We'll see about that tomorrow morning. ...'

And Monsieur Martin followed the young man, labouring under the weight of his luggage. He had never imagined such a long platform. It was like an endless, deserted racecourse, with a row of mysterious doors alongside it.

Finally the young man pushed open the last door.

'Come in!'

It was dark. Nothing but a lamp with a green shade, hanging so low over the table that it only shone on a few papers. Something was stirring, however, in the depths of the room.

'Good evening, Monsieur Martin!...' said a friendly voice.

And an enormous figure emerged from the shadows: Inspector Maigret, huddled in his heavy velvet-collared overcoat, his hands in his pockets.

'Don't bother to put them down. We're going to take the train to Paris, which is just coming in on Platform Three....'

This time there was no doubt about it: Martin was weeping silently, his hands immobilized by his beautifully-arranged suitcases.

The detective who had been stationed at 61 Place des Vosges had telephoned Maigret a few hours previously:

'Our man's on the run.... He took a taxi and asked to be driven to the Gare du Nord....'

'Let him run.... Keep watching the woman....'

And Maigret had taken the same train as Martin. He had travelled in the next compartment, with two N.C.O.s who had told ribald stories the whole way.

From time to time, the Inspector had put his eye to the little peephole between the two compartments, and caught sight of Martin looking gloomy.

Jeumont.... Identity cards!... The Special Inspector's office.

Now they were both travelling back to Paris in a reserved compartment. Martin was not handcuffed. His suitcases were on the rack above his head, and one of them, precariously balanced, looked like tumbling down on him.

At Maubeuge, Maigret had not yet asked him a single question.

It was uncanny! He was wedged in his corner with his pipe between his teeth. He never stopped smoking, watching his companion with little twinkling eyes.

A dozen times, a score of times Martin had opened his

mouth without bringing himself to speak. A dozen times, a score of times the Inspector had taken no notice.

It happened at last, however; a voice beyond description, which Madame Martin herself would probably not have recognized.

'It was I . . .'

And Maigret still uttered no word. His eyes seemed to be saying: Really?

'I . . . I was hoping to cross the frontier. . . .'

There is a certain way of smoking that is exasperating to whoever watches the smoker: at every puff the lips part voluptuously with a tiny *poc*. And the smoke, instead of flying forward, escapes slowly, forming a cloud round the face.

Maigret was smoking like that, and his head was swaying from right to left, from left to right, to the rhythm of the train.

Martin was leaning forward, his gloved hands painfully tense and his eyes feverish.

'D'you think it'll be a long business? . . . It won't, will it? since I'm confessing. . . . For I confess everything. . . .'

How did he manage not to break into sobs? Every nerve must have been strained. And from time to time his eyes wore an imploring look, saying clearly to Maigret: 'Please help me! You see I'm at the end of my tether! . . .'

But the Inspector did not budge. He was as placid, with the same interested but dispassionate look, as if he had been in a zoo, in front of the cage of some exotic animal.

'Couchet caught me . . . so then. . . .'

And Maigret sighed. A sigh that meant nothing, or rather that could be interpreted in a hundred different ways.

Saint-Quentin! Footsteps in the corridor. A stout traveller tried to open the door of the compartment, discovered that it was fastened, stopped for a moment looking in with his nose pressed against the window, and at last resigned himself to looking for a seat elsewhere.

'As I'm confessing everything, surely? . . . It's not worth trying to deny . . .'

He might just as well have been speaking to a deaf man, or to someone who did not know a word of French. Maigret was filling his pipe, prodding it meticulously with his forefinger.

'Have you any matches?'

'No . . . I don't smoke. . . . You know I don't. . . . It's because my wife doesn't like the smell of tobacco. . . . I'd like it to be over quickly, d'you understand? . . . I shall say so to the lawyer I shall have to choose. . . . No complications! . . . I'll confess everything! . . . I read in the paper that they've found some of the notes. . . . I don't know why I did that. . . . Knowing I'd got them in my pocket, I felt as if everybody in the street was staring at me. . . . At first I thought of hiding them somewhere. . . . But what for? . . .

'I walked along the embankment. . . . There were some barges. . . . I was afraid of being seen by a boatman. . . .

'Then I crossed the Pont-Marie and on the Île Saint-Louis I was able to get rid of the bundle. . . .'

The compartment was very hot. Steam was trickling down the panes. Tobacco smoke was wreathing round the lamp.

'I should have confessed it all the first time I saw you. . . . I hadn't the courage. . . . I was hoping that . . .'

Martin fell silent, and stared in surprise at his companion, whose mouth had fallen open and whose eyes were closed. His breathing was as regular as the purring of a big, satisfied cat!

Maigret was asleep!

The other man cast a glance towards the door, which only needed pushing. And as if to avoid the temptation, he huddled in a corner, his thighs pressed tightly together, his two frantic hands on his bony knees.

The Gare du Nord. A grey morning. And the crowd of suburban travellers, still only half awake, trooping out through the gates.

The train had stopped a long way from the main hall. The cases were heavy. Martin was unwilling to stop. He was breathless and both his arms were aching.

They had to wait a longish time for a taxi.

'Are you taking me to jail?'

They had spent five hours in the train and Maigret had not spoken more than a dozen sentences. And even those were sentences that had nothing to do with the crime, nor with the three hundred and sixty thousand francs! He had talked about his pipe, or the heat, or the time the train was due in.

'61 Place des Vosges!' he said to the taxi driver.

Martin begged him:

'Do you think it's necessary to . . .'

And to himself:

'What must they be thinking at the office? I hadn't time to let them know. . . .'

In her lodge, the concierge was sorting the mail: a great pile of letters for the Serum laboratory, a tiny pile for the rest of the house.

'Monsieur Martin! Monsieur Martin! . . . They called round from the Wills and Probate to find out if you were ill. . . . It seems you've got the key of . . .'

Maigret hurried his companion forward. And the latter had to drag his heavy cases up the stairs, where milk bottles and loaves of bread were standing in front of the doors.

Old Mathilde's door was seen to move.

'Give me the key.'

'But . . .'

'Open it yourself.'

A deep silence. The click of the lock. Then the orderly dining-room was seen, with everything in its proper place.

Martin hesitated for a long time before saying, in a loud voice:

'It's me!... And the Inspector....'

Somebody stirred in bed in the next room. As he closed the door behind him, Martin moaned:

'We shouldn't have ... She's not involved in this, is she? ... And in her condition....'

He dared not go in to the bedroom. To keep himself in countenance he picked up his suitcases and laid them on two chairs.

'Shall I make some coffee?'

Maigret was knocking at the bedroom door.

'May I come in?'

No answer. He pushed open the door, and Madame Martin's stare met him full in the face, as she lay there motionless, with her hair in pins.

'Excuse me for disturbing you.... I've brought back your husband, who made the mistake of panicking....'

Martin was behind him. He could feel him there, but not see him.

Footsteps rang out in the courtyard, and voices, particularly women's voices: the office and laboratory staff were arriving. It was one minute to nine.

A stifled cry from the madwoman next door. Bottles of medicine on the bedside table.

'Are you feeling worse?'

He knew she would not answer, that she would keep up the same tense, guarded attitude in spite of everything.

It seemed as if she was afraid of a word, of a single word! As if one word might have let loose disasters!

She had grown thinner. Her complexion was more ashen.

But the eyes, those strange grey eyes, still retained their own burning, self-willed vitality.

Martin came in, weak-kneed. His whole attitude seemed apologetic, begging for forgiveness.

The grey eyes turned slowly towards him, with a look so hard and frozen that he averted his head, muttering:

'It was at Jeumont station. . . . One minute more and I'd have been in Belgium. . . .'

Words were needed, sentences, noise, to fill the emptiness that could be felt surrounding each person. An emptiness which was so palpable that their voices seemed to echo as if in a tunnel or a cave.

But nobody talked. They uttered a few syllables, painfully, with anxious glances, then silence fell again, implacable as a fog.

Something was happening, none the less. Something slow and stealthy: a hand was creeping out from under the covers and moving imperceptibly towards the pillow.

The thin, damp hand of Madame Martin. Maigret, although looking the other way, was watching its progress, waiting for the moment when that hand would finally reach its goal.

'Isn't the doctor coming this morning?'

'I don't know. . . . Is anybody looking after me? . . . I'm here like an animal left to die. . . .'

But her eyes brightened as her hand at last touched the object she was seeking.

A barely perceptible rustle of paper.

Maigret took one step forward, seized Madame Martin by the wrist. She seemed to be devoid of strength, almost devoid of life. None the less within the space of one second she gave proof of incredible energy.

What she held, she had no intention of relinquishing. Sitting up in bed, she defended herself furiously. She raised her hand to her mouth. With her teeth, she tore the white sheet of paper she was clutching.

'Let go of me! ... Let go or I'll scream! ... And *you* just stand by and watch him! ...'

'Please, Inspector ... I implore you. ...' Martin was moaning.

He was listening anxiously. He was afraid of all the other tenants rushing in. He dared not intervene.

'You brute! ... You foul brute! ... Striking a woman!'

No, Maigret did not strike her. He merely grasped her hand, gripping the wrist rather tightly maybe, to prevent her from destroying the paper.

'Aren't you ashamed? ... A woman at death's door. ...'

A woman who was displaying energy the like of which Maigret had rarely encountered during the whole of his career in the police! His bowler hat fell on the bed. She suddenly bit him on the wrist.

But with her nerves so strained she could not last out much longer, and he managed to part her fingers, while she uttered a moan of pain.

Now she was weeping! She was weeping without tears, from resentment, from rage, perhaps also for the sake of striking an attitude?

'And *you* let him do it. ...'

Maigret's back was too broad for the narrow room. It seemed to fill up the whole space, to shut out the light.

He went to the fireplace, unfolded the sheet of paper, the ends of which were torn off, and ran his eyes over a type-written document surmounted by the heading:

Maîtres Laval and Piollet,
Consultant Solicitors,
Paris

On the right, in red letters: *Couchet/Martin Case. Consultation of 16 November.*

Two pages of dense typescript, single-spaced. Maigret read only scraps of it, half aloud, and the rattle of typewriters could be heard from the offices of the Serum laboratory.

In view of the law of . . .

Given the fact that the death of Roger Couchet was subsequent to that of his father . . .

. . . that no will can deprive a legitimate son of the share to which he is entitled . . .

. . . that in the case of the second marriage of the testator, to Madame Couchet née Dormoy, all goods were held in common . . .

. . . that the natural heir of Roger Couchet is his mother . . .

. . . have the honour to inform you that you are entitled to claim one half of the fortune left by Raymond Couchet, his goods and chattels and his real estate . . . which, according to our private information we estimate, subject to error, at about five million francs, the value of the firm known as Dr Rivière's Serums being reckoned in this estimate as three million . . .

. . . We are entirely at your disposal for any steps required for the annulment of the will and . . .

. . . We confirm our statement that we shall retain a commission of ten per cent for expenses on the sums thus recovered . . .

Madame Martin had stopped crying. She was lying down again, and her cold gaze fixed once more on the ceiling.

Martin was standing in the doorway, more distracted than ever, not knowing what to do with his hands, with his eyes, with his whole body.

'There's a postscript!' the Inspector muttered to himself.

This postscript was preceded by a note: *Strictly confidential.*

We have reason to believe that Madame Couchet, née Dormoy, is also prepared to contest the will. Furthermore, we have made inquiries concerning the third legatee, Nine Moinard. This person

*is a woman of questionable respectability, who has hitherto taken
no steps to claim her rights. Seeing that she is at present without
means, it appears to us that the most expedient plan is to offer her
some sum by way of compensation. For our part, we would estimate
such a sum at twenty thousand francs, which is likely to attract a
person in Mademoiselle Moinard's position.*

We await your decision on this matter.

Maigret's pipe had gone out. Slowly, he refolded the
paper and slipped it into his wallet.

Around him, utter silence reigned. Martin was holding
his breath. His wife, lying on the bed with her fixed stare,
looked as if she were already dead.

'Two million five hundred thousand francs . . .' muttered
the Inspector. 'Less the twenty thousand to be given Nine
so that she should prove accommodating. . . . It's true that
Madame Couchet will probably pay half of that. . . .'

He was convinced that a smile of triumph, barely perceptible and yet eloquent, passed over the woman's lips.

'It's quite a sum! . . . Tell me, Martin . . .'

The latter started, tried to stand on the defensive.

'How much do you expect to get? . . . I'm not referring
to money . . . I'm talking about your sentence. . . . Robbery.
. . . Murder. . . . Perhaps they'll prove premeditation. . . .
What's your guess? . . . No question of acquittal, of course,
since it's not a crime of passion. . . . Oh, if only your wife
had renewed relations with her former husband. . . . But
that wasn't the case. . . . A question of money, pure and
simple. . . . Ten years? Twenty years? . . . D'you want my
opinion? . . .

'Notice that one can never forecast the average judge's
decision. . . .

'All the same, there are precedents. . . . Well, one may
say that as a general rule, while they're indulgent about

129

crimes of passion, they show the utmost severity when money's the motive. . . .'

He seemed to be talking for the sake of talking, to gain time.

'It's quite understandable! They are middle-class people themselves, businessmen. . . . They think they've got nothing to fear as regards mistresses: either they've got none, or they're sure of them. . . . But they've got everything to fear from thieves. . . . Twenty years? . . . Well, no! . . . I'd be more inclined to say the death penalty. . . .'

Martin had stopped moving now. He looked even more ghastly than his wife. He was forced to cling to the doorpost for support.

'Only Madame Martin will be a rich woman. . . . She's reached an age when one knows how to enjoy life and wealth. . . .'

He went closer to the window.

'Except that this window . . . This is the stumbling-block. They won't fail to point out that from here, everything could have been seen. . . . Everything, you hear! . . . And that's a serious matter! . . . Because it might involve the question of complicity. . . . Now in the Code there's a small item that debars the murderer, even if he's acquitted, from inheriting from his victim. . . . Not only the murderer. . . . His accomplices. . . . You see why this window's so important. . . .'

It was no longer merely silence that reigned around him. It was something more absolute, more disturbing, almost unreal: a total absence of life.

And then a sudden question:

'Tell me, Martin! What did you do with the gun?'

Something living stirred in the passage: old Mathilde, evidently, with her moon face, her flabby stomach under a check apron.

The shrill voice of the concierge, in the courtyard:

'Madame Martin! ... It's from Dufayel's! ...'

Maigret sat down in an easy chair which groaned, but did not collapse immediately.

Chapter 11

The Drawing on the Wall

'Answer me! ... That gun. ...'

He followed Martin's gaze and noticed that Madame Martin, whose eyes were still fixed on the ceiling, was moving her fingers against the wall.

Poor Martin was making incredible efforts to understand what she was trying to tell him. He was growing impatient. He could see that Maigret was waiting.

'I ...'

What could be the meaning of that square, or trapezium, that she was tracing with her skinny finger?

'Well?'

At that moment, Maigret felt really sorry for him. It must have been a terrible minute. Martin was gasping with impatience.

'I threw it into the Seine. ...'

The die was cast! As the Inspector drew the revolver from his pocket and laid it on the table, Madame Martin sat bolt upright in her bed, looking like a fury.

'Well, *I* eventually found it in the dustbin. ...' said Maigret.

And then the hoarse voice of the sick woman:

'There! ... D'you understand now? ... Are you pleased with yourself? ... You've missed your chance, once again, as you've missed all your chances! ... As if you'd done it on purpose, for fear of going to prison. ... But you'll go to prison all the same! ... For the robbery was *your* job! ...

The three hundred and sixty notes that Monsieur threw into the Seine ...'

She was terrifying. It was clear that she had held herself back too long. The reaction was savage. And her excitement was so intense that sometimes several words rose to her lips at the same time, and she uttered the syllables confusedly. ...

Martin hung his head. His part was played. His wife's accusation was true, he had failed lamentably.

'... Monsieur takes it into his head to be a thief, but he leaves his glove on the table. ...'

All Madame Martin's grievances were going to pour forth, pell-mell.

Behind him, Maigret heard the meek voice of the man in the buff overcoat.

'For months she'd been showing me the office through the window, and Couchet going off to the toilet. ... And she blamed me for making her life a misery, and for being incapable of providing for a wife. ... I went down there ...'

'Did you tell her you were going?'

'No! But she knew quite well I was. She was at the window. ...'

'And you saw, from a distance, that your husband had left his glove behind, Madame Martin?'

'As if he'd left his visiting card! He might have done it on purpose to infuriate me. ...'

'You took your revolver and you went down there. ... Couchet came in while you were in the office. ... He thought it was you who had robbed him. ...'

'He wanted to have me arrested. Yes, indeed! that's what he wanted to do! As if it wasn't thanks to me that he'd grown rich! ... Who was it that looked after him in the early days, when he barely made enough to live on dry bread? ... And men are all the same! ... He even re-proached me for living in the house where he had his office. ... He accused me of sharing in the money he gave my son. ...'

'And you fired?'

'He'd already lifted the telephone to call the police!'

'You went along to the dustbins. Under pretext of looking for a lost spoon you buried the revolver in the rubbish. ... Who did you meet then? ...'

She spat out:

'The old fool from the first floor. ...'

'Nobody else? ... I thought your son had come. ... He had no more money. ...'

'And so what? ...'

'He'd not come to see you, but his father, isn't that so? Only you couldn't let him go into the office, where he would have discovered the body ... You were in the courtyard, both of you. ... What did you tell Roger?'

'To go away. ... You cannot understand a mother's feelings. ...'

'And he went off. ... Your husband came back. ... Nothing was said. ... Am I right? Martin was thinking about the notes he had finally thrown into the Seine, since at heart the poor fellow's not a bad sort. ...'

'The poor fellow's not a bad sort!' repeated Madame Martin with unexpected fury. 'Ha! Ha! ... And what about me? ... Me, who've always been unlucky. ...'

'Martin doesn't know who's done the murder. ... He goes to bed. A whole day goes by without anything being said. ... But, the following night, you get up to hunt through the clothes he's taken off. ... You look in vain for the notes. ... He watches you. You question him. And then comes the storm of rage that old Mathilde overheard from behind the door. ... You've committed a murder for nothing! That idiot Martin has thrown away the notes! ...

A whole fortune in the Seine, just for lack of guts! . . . It makes you ill. . . . You become feverish. . . . While Martin, not knowing that you were the murderer, goes off to tell the news to Roger. . . .

'And Roger understands. He'd seen you in the courtyard. . . . You'd prevented him from going further. . . . He knows you well. . . .

'He believes I suspect him. . . . He imagines he's going to be arrested, accused. . . . And he cannot defend himself without accusing his mother. . . .

'He wasn't a very attractive young man, maybe. . . . But there's surely some excuse for his way of life. . . . He's sick of it all . . . sick of the women he goes to bed with, of drugs, of his wasted life in Montmartre and, on top of everything, of this family melodrama, of which he alone can guess all the motives. . . .

'He jumps out of the window!'

Martin was leaning against the wall, his face in his folded arms. But his wife was staring fixedly at the Inspector, as if she were just waiting for the moment to interrupt his story and attack in her turn.

Then Maigret showed the letter from the two lawyers.

'On my last visit, Martin was so frightened that he was about to confess his theft. . . . But you were there. . . . He could see you through the crack of the door. . . . You made violent signs and he held his tongue . . .

'Wasn't that what finally opened his eyes? . . . He questions you. . . . Yes, you killed Couchet! You shout it in his face! You killed Couchet because of him, to cover up his mistake, because of that glove left on Couchet's desk! And because you killed him, you won't inherit, in spite of the will! . . . Oh, if only Martin were a man. . . .

'He must go abroad. . . . He'll be thought guilty. . . . The police won't bother you and you'll go and join him, with Couchet's millions. . . .

'Poor old Martin! ...'

And Maigret almost crushed the little fellow with a tremendous pat on the shoulder. He had kept his voice low. He let his words fall without stress.

'To have done so much for the sake of that money! Couchet's death.... Roger throwing himself out of the window ... and to realize at the last minute that one's not going to get it! ... You insisted on preparing Martin's luggage yourself.... Neatly packed suitcases.... Enough linen for several months....'

'Stop!' implored Martin.

The madwoman howled. Maigret opened the door suddenly and old Mathilde nearly fell forward!

She fled, frightened by the Inspector's tone, and for the first time she shut her door properly, turning the key in the lock.

Maigret cast a last glance into the room. Martin was too terrified to move. His wife, sitting up in bed, thin, her shoulder-blades protruding under her nightgown, followed the detective with her eyes.

She had suddenly become so grave, so calm, that they wondered anxiously what she was planning.

Maigret remembered certain glances during the scene that had just taken place, the way her lips had twitched. And just the same moment as Martin, he realized intuitively what was happening.

They could do nothing about it. It took place outside of them, like a bad dream.

Madame Martin was very, very thin. And her features became even more anguished. What was she looking at, in places where there was nothing but the ordinary objects of her bedroom?

What was she following so attentively through the room?

Her brow grew furrowed. Her temples were throbbing. Martin cried out:

'I'm frightened!'

Nothing had changed in the flat. A lorry made its way into the courtyard and the shrill voice of the concierge could be heard.

It seemed as if Madame Martin was making a tremendous effort, all alone, to climb an inaccessible mountain. Twice she gestured vaguely with her hand as though brushing away something from her face. At last she gulped, and then smiled like someone who has reached the goal:

'You'll all end by coming to ask me for a little money. . . . I shall tell my lawyer not to give you any. . . .'

Martin shook from head to foot. He understood that this was no passing delirium brought on by fever.

She had definitely gone out of her mind!

'You can't blame her. She's never been quite like other people, has she? . . .' he moaned.

He was waiting for the Inspector to agree with him.

'Poor old Martin. . . .'

Martin was weeping! He had taken hold of his wife's hand and was rubbing his face against it. She repulsed him. She was wearing a superior, scornful smile.

'Not more than five francs at a time . . . I've suffered enough in my time from . . .'

'I'll go and telephone St Anne's Hospital. . . .' said Maigret.

'D'you think so? . . . Must . . . must she be shut up?'

Force of habit? Martin was panicking at the thought of leaving his home, that atmosphere of daily nagging and bickering, that sordid life, that woman who, for the last time, was trying to think but who lay back, discouraged and defeated, heaving a great sigh and mumbling:

'Bring me the key . . .'

A few minutes later Maigret was crossing the crowded streets like a stranger. He had an appalling headache, a thing that rarely happened to him, and he went into a chemist's shop to swallow an aspirin.

He saw nothing of what was going on around him. The noises in the street were intermingled with others, with voices particularly, that went on echoing in his head.

One picture haunted him more than the rest: Madame Martin getting up, picking her husband's clothes off the floor, and hunting for the money! And Martin watching her from his bed!

The woman's questioning look:

'*I threw them into the Seine....*'

It was from that moment that something had cracked. Or rather, she had always been slightly unhinged! Even when she was living in the confectioner's shop at Meaux!

Only then it was not noticeable. She was a girl, and almost a pretty one! Nobody worried if her lips were too thin....

And Couchet married her!

'What would become of me if anything happened to you?'

Maigret had to wait, to cross the Boulevard Beaumarchais. For no reason, he thought of Nine.

'She'll get nothing! Not a penny ...' he murmured below his breath. 'The will is sure to be declared invalid. And it's Madame Couchet, *née* Dormoy ...'

The Colonel had probably started proceedings. That was only natural. Madame Couchet would get it all! All those millions....

Madame Couchet was a lady, and would know how to live like one....

Maigret slowly climbed the stairs and opened the door of the flat in the Boulevard Richard-Lenoir.

'Guess who's come?'

Madame Maigret was laying four places on the white

tablecloth. On the sideboard, Maigret noticed a bottle of plum brandy.

'Your sister!'

It wasn't hard to guess, since every time she came from Alsace she brought a bottle of fruit liqueur and a smoked ham.

'She's gone to do a few errands with André....'

Her husband: a worthy fellow who ran a brickfield.

'You're looking tired ... I hope you're not going out any more today, are you?'

Maigret did not go out again. At nine o'clock that evening he was playing Pope Joan with his sister and brother-in-law. The dining-room was redolent of plum brandy.

And Madame Maigret kept breaking into fits of laughter because she was no card-player and made the silliest mistakes imaginable.

'You're sure you've not got a nine?'

'Yes, I have....'

'Well then, why don't you play it?'

To Maigret, it was all as soothing as a warm bath. He had lost his headache.

He had stopped thinking about Madame Martin, who was being carried in an ambulance to St Anne's Hospital, while her husband sobbed all by himself on the empty staircase.

More about Penguins

Penguinews, which appears every month, contains details of all the new books issued by Penguins as they are published. From time to time it is supplemented by *Penguins in Print*, which is a complete list of all books published by Penguins which are in print. (There are well over three thousand of these.)

A specimen copy of *Penguinews* will be sent to you free on request, and you can become a subscriber for the price of the postage. For a year's issues (including the complete lists) please send 30p if you live in the United Kingdom, or 60p if you live elsewhere. Just write to Dept EP, Penguin Books Ltd, Harmondsworth, Middlesex, enclosing a cheque or postal order, and your name will be added to the mailing list.

Other Penguins by Simenon are described on the following pages.

Note: *Penguinews* and *Penguins in Print* are not available in the U.S.A. or Canada

A New Lease of Life

Guilt worked like a poison
in the mind of Maurice Dudon, lonely Paris bachelor. A
creeping invisible sense of blame coloured his relations with
women, his attitude to money, everything about his life.

No wonder, then, that when he thought he had struck a
vein of genuine love – with the woman who nursed him back
to health after his car accident – the promise of a new lease
of life should seem, at first, so real, and should turn sour
on him so quickly...

Here is Simenon's X-ray psychological insight at its most
penetrating.

Not for Sale in the U.S.A. or Canada

Also available

Stranger in the House
Ticket of Leave

Not for sale in the U.S.A.

and

The Patient
Sunday

Not for sale in the U.S.A. or Canada

Some Simenon Crime

'The best living detective-writer . . . Maigret is the very bloodhound of heaven' – C. Day Lewis in a broadcast

Some of the Simenon crime available in Penguins:

Maigret Meets a Milord
Maigret and the Hundred Gibbets
Maigret and the Enigmatic Lett
Maigret Stonewalled
Maigret at the Crossroads
Maigret Mystified

Also available in the U.K. but not for sale in the U.S.A. or Canada:

Maigret has Scruples
Maigret's First Case
Maigret Sets a Trap
Maigret Loses his Temper
Maigret and the Lazy Burglar
Maigret and the Saturday Caller
The Iron Staircase
The Door
Maigret's Memoirs
Account Unsettled
The Blue Room
The Fate of the Malous
Murderer
The Third Simenon Omnibus*
The Fourth Simenon Omnibus

*Not for sale in the U.S.A. only